The Wayward Soul

GEORGE FLORES

Firestorm Press
PO BOX 493514
Garland, TX 75049

www.georgeflores.us

Cover by Graphicz X Designs
http://graphiczxdesigns.zenfolio.com

Library of Congress Control Number: 2015937287
Firestorm Press, Garland, TX

ISBN-13: 978-0-692-40645-8 (paperback)
ISBN-13: 978-0-692-41271-8 (eBook)

Acknowledgments

Thank you to my wife, Gloria, and my son, Matthew, for your love and unyielding support. To the rest of my family, I love you all. Thank you, Mike, for your help and words of encouragement. A special "thank you" to MJ, you did a wonderful job! To Donald, for sharing your insight which helped contribute to this story. Thank you.

Acknowledgments

Thank you to my wife, Gloria, and my son, Matthew, for your love and unyielding support. To the rest of my family, I love you all. Thank you, Mike, for your help and words of encouragement. A special "thank you" to MJ, you did a wonderful job! To Donald, for sharing your insight which helped contribute to this story. Thank you.

For C. G.

The Wayward Soul

ONE

Adam strolled past a group of freshmen in the hallway. They were small. Smaller than the ones the year before—a trend, it appeared to Adam, who didn't consider himself as being tall to begin with. He was content being average height, a means by which he blended in, as being tall meant being popular, something he wasn't, and being popular meant having cool hair and nice clothes, of which he had neither.

At the end of the hallway, he turned to face the lockers that lined the wall, then he swung his backpack off his shoulders and it dropped to his feet. He opened his locker and stood there figuring out which books he'd need. A few students brushed past him, heading for their lockers nearby.

A muscular arm sprung out at Adam, who caught the open palm in a loud *pop!* that served as a handshake from his friend Dave.

"You going to Natalie's party tonight?" Dave arched his tongue and nodded slowly to show his enthusiasm.

Adam let go of Dave's hand. "I don't know." He dug around in his locker searching through binders and a messy pile of loose-leaf papers, then grabbed a yellow and green bound book he would need for his Algebra class and slid it into his backpack.

"I have to work tonight." Adam slung the backpack over one shoulder, then the next.

"Her parents are out of town. We're gonna get tore up!" Dave assured him, smiling. He made a quick transaction at his locker next to Adam's, then shut the door with a slam and tapped Adam on the shoulder as he walked past him.

"I don't know. I'll see you at lunch," Adam called out to Dave, who had begun down the hallway where he caught up to his girlfriend, Natalie.

Valery stood in front of her open locker. She had been a friend of Adam's since their elementary school days.

"Are you going?" she asked.

"Why? You want to come?"

"You know I'm not allowed to stay out late," Valery shot back in an irksome tone.

John stood one locker away from Valery. He fingered his combination lock, then pulled the little handle and opened the door. Proceeding silently, he seemed to ignore the world around him as he rummaged through the clutter.

Adam watched Valery suddenly stand back, and with a giddy, loud voice, she said, "Do you know what yesterday was?"

"ER night," Adam said, topped with a sigh. One of the networks ran ER reruns on Thursday nights, and every Friday morning Valery asked Adam if he'd watched the show.

Valery clasped her hands together, as if to thank the heavens above, looked up, and in a spellbound manner, said, "George Clooney is sooo sexy."

"Calm down, Valery," said Andrew, an Asian student gathering his things from a locker nearby.

The bell chimed, meaning it was now 8:45 a.m. and a rush of students swarmed the hallway.

"I've got to run. See you in Mrs. Ellison's class, okay?" Valery said with an easy smile.

"Okay, bye, Val," Adam said.

"Bye, John." She peeked over at John with a little wave.

John made a feeble attempt to wave back, without looking away from his locker.

Valery left, and Adam watched as she walked away.

Adam turned to look at John, who was taking loose papers out of his locker and organizing his books and binders. Watching him move slowly, Adam waited for what seemed like several minutes.

"Let's go, John."

John paused; he looked at Adam just long enough to show his lack of concern, then went back to stowing away.

Adam hung around near the staircase, occasionally glancing down, and waited until he heard the clank of the locker door shutting, followed by a series of noises indicating that John had locked up his things.

They headed down the stairs, then walked down a hall that was empty except for a girl pulling a black-wheeled case, but she, too, disappeared through an open door.

Adam had continued straight but changed directions and followed John as he meandered into the restroom.

John threw his backpack onto the counter and

stood in front of the mirror. He leaned forward to get a closer look at his eyes, then began to pull some things out of his backpack. First, he took out a small bottle and a contact lens container from one of the pockets, then placed both items next to one of the sinks. He turned on the water and reached for the soap dispenser, giving it a couple pumps.

"I wouldn't do that," Adam called out as he made his way to one of the urinals where he unzipped his pants.

John looked back at him through the mirror. "Why?"

Adam waited until he was done, then turned around and zipped up. He didn't flush—Adam never liked touching the flushing handles in public restrooms. He also kept in mind to avoid the soap dispenser as he went to use the sink next to John's.

"The other day, Dave took a half-empty soap container out of one of the dispensers. He went into a stall and when he came back, it was full," Adam said.

"That's gross. Why would he do something like that? Doesn't he know some of us like to wash our hands?"

"Yeah, he knows; he just doesn't care. He's a senior. He feels it's his job to leave his mark, I guess. Don't you feel like you don't care anymore? We're seniors!"

"Yeah, but I don't go around peeing in the soap."

Adam looked at himself in the mirror. The chinos he wore were starting to show their age, but they didn't stand out as much as the dark t-shirt he suddenly realized needed ironing. No one would notice, he thought, then watched John insert his contacts.

John put his eye-care products away, then gave his hair one last look of approval and strapped on his backpack.

"You know what else he did?" Adam said as they exited the restroom. "Remember, a couple of weeks ago, when we had that egg-drop? Mr. Norton sent a couple of us to go clean out the containers. Well, Dave came in. He sucked some egg-white into his mouth, then spit it out on the toilet seats and the walls of the bathroom stalls."

John smiled, but shook his head resentfully.

They arrived at their classroom, and John made his way to the back and found a seat.

Adam sat next to the teacher's desk, not by his own volition, but he seemed to be making progress. He adjusted himself, finding it difficult to get comfortable in the hard plastic chair with a steal bar arched over the backrest intended to jab those in the back threatening to slouch.

Mrs. Freud walked in carrying a tray from the cafeteria. The room filled with the smell of sausage and syrup. She balanced the tray on one hand, managing to carry her change-purse in the other. A bottled soft drink hung from between her crooked fingers. She placed her food down on her desk, grabbed her giant gasoline-station mug, and walked back out.

Adam went to visit Anthony, the introverted skater with a rocker guise who was pantomiming and laughing as he spoke to Mike, a student who sat beside him. All Adam managed to hear was, "And I didn't clear it, then *bam!* I busted my shin on the pavement." Mike and Anthony laughed.

"Hey, Anthony, let me see your calculator," Adam said. "You still got that drug dealer game on it?"

Anthony reached into his backpack. "One time I made it twenty-five days—almost forty Gs, until the cops busted me." He unzipped a few compartments somewhere inside, then handed Adam the scientific calculator. Anthony turned to face Mike and they continued talking.

Adam went back to his desk. He turned on the

calculator, and then, for a moment, he looked up.

BUS 1311 IS RUNNING LATE!

NATURE AND WILDLIFE CLUB
MEETING AT 4:30
ROOM 304

DEBATE TEAM MEETS IN COMMONS
MON-THURS MORN.

CHESS CLUB COMPETITION SATURDAY!

9:15:16

The words flashed continuously on a television screen cornered above Mrs. Freud's desk.

Mrs. Freud returned a few minutes later with her mug full of ice. She opened her drink and poured herself some soda, and as it settled, she bit into her breakfast. Somewhere under a mesh of worksheets on her desk, the phone rang.

"Yes?" She removed her glasses and rubbed the bridge of her nose, then rested her arms on the desk.

"What happened?"

"Well, is he alright?"

"Thank the Lord. Is he there? Can I speak with him?"

The sound of crackling ice could be heard in the quiet room as Mrs. Freud took a long drink from her oversized mug. She gulped, then set the mug back on her desk. The person on the other end did most of the talking. As she listened, she turned her chair away from the class.

"I had to step out briefly. Is he okay?"

"Can you put him on?" She caged her hair in one hand, leaving it a disheveled mess as she moved her hand back down.

"Are you okay, Benny? Did they hurt you?"

"Do you want to go home?"

"Okay, put Principal Mackey back on."

"I think it'd be best if you allowed my son to go home. He's been suffering from a great deal of emotional stress. He can collect his work and do it at home—he's a good kid, he'll be fine. He probably just needs a little time."

Everyone listened.

"Well, it sounds like someone should've been there. He's only a third-grader; those boys should know better."

"Okay, I hope so."

She spoke to her son again.

"Mr. Mackey is going to let you go home. Ask Mrs. Bryan for make-up work, and call me when you get home. Be careful, Benjamin. Don't cross the big street unless you see the 'walk' sign, and remember to look both ways first."

She listened tolerantly before she said, "Okay, I appreciate it, Mr. Mackey. Thank you for notifying me. Goodbye."

She slapped her forehead, then reached inside a desk drawer where she kept a large bottle of Aspirin. A few shakes of the bottle over an open palm produced two little pills that she popped into her mouth to be whisked away with soda. She rubbed the bridge of her nose a couple more times, then finished her breakfast.

After she finished, Mrs. Freud wiped her hands and mouth on a napkin. She started her computer, and while waiting for it come on, stacked some papers on her desk.

Going about their own, the students were scattered throughout the classroom working on an assignment. The assignment numbers had been listed on the dry-erase board, and the class followed along on their open math books.

Edward, a quiet student, raised his hand and

waited politely until Mrs. Freud became aware of him sitting in the middle row.

"Yes, Edward?"

"I don't get it," Edward said, looking down at his paper.

"What don't you understand?"

"Number three on section twelve."

Mrs. Freud stood from her desk carrying her book. She flipped through pages to find the problem in question, then turned to face the dry-erase board and popped the lid off one of the markers; she began to draw a parallelogram, but stopped. "Well, I guess you'd need a protractor to measure the angles. Omit that one." An eraser went up. "But I'll explain how you work the problem anyway."

Edward watched attentively while the students nearby finished their conversations, then began to quiet down.

Mrs. Freud carefully drew the shape again, marking several points along the sides as she explained.

"Now, imagine you have a flat plane . . ." She labeled the points X1, X2, B, C, and D.

"What I don't understand is the flat plane." Adam looked down at his hands preoccupied with the scientific calculator, stealthily pecking at it while inside the desk compartment.

Mrs. Freud stopped and turned to face Adam. She crossed her arms and shifted her weight over to one leg.

Adam looked up to find an impaling stare antipathetically awaiting further explanation.

"A flat plane is a two-dimensional shape with a length and a width, an area but no height," she said sternly.

"Hmm, but, just because something appears to be flat, doesn't mean it's without three dimensions," Adam rebuked. "To us, it appears flat, but if you were to shrink us somehow, it would increase the size of the plane to where it would then be wider than us, giving it some height—regardless of how small it appeared before."

Laughter erupted throughout the room.

"Hey, yeah, Mrs. Freud," said Mark, another student.

Adam glanced back to see delirious faces and a spectrum of wide smiles.

Mrs. Freud bowed her head, devising a solution. She looked back up and stared at him, sizing him up before exiting the room.

Seconds after it was clear she was gone, the

classroom filled with boisterous chatter.

"She doesn't know what she's doing."

"How did she get this job?"

"I hope she gets fired."

"Let's put some Ex-Lax in her drink."

Mark came over and stood near the front row. "Whoa, Adam, you made her look stupid."

Adam knew what was coming, and he had no choice but to wait at his desk, procuring a sly smile to mask his angst for what would be the imminent conviction of Mrs. Freud's contretemps.

Red flashes of fury ignited across her face as she rushed back in, stopping halfway between Adam and the classroom entrance.

"Get your things. Come on, let's go!" She motioned a few circles with the flick of her wrist, then stood outside the door with her chin up and chest out, like a soldier at attention.

Adam dropped the calculator into his backpack before he stood. He flung the backpack over one shoulder and the door slammed the moment he stepped into the hallway.

Only the words, "You're going to Mr. Ford's office," were said.

There was no sense in trying to explain, or even reason with her.

Mr. Ford's office was across the hall—the corner office.

Properly escorting Adam, Mrs. Freud held the door open and asked him to take a seat in the waiting area, where two glass walls formed a corner.

Adam sat on one of the plush office chairs. Mrs. Freud stormed off down the hallway without saying a word to the receptionist.

The receptionist sat behind an L-shaped counter reviewing attendance sheets, sitting quietly until she answered the phone. The spade leaves of a small plant sitting on the counter were all Adam could see of the reception desk. To his side, the wooden table cornered between the rows of seats displayed various school-related brochures. Adam looked through the glass at the empty hall, resentfully thinking about the smart remark that had landed him in the office.

He heard voices nearby and assumed Mr. Ford's door had been open.

"Damn it, Barbra! I can't just stop what I'm doing because somebody questioned your abilities."

Maybe it won't be so bad after all, Adam thought. Just last week, Mrs. Freud had sent Adam to the counselor's office for looking up pornography on the Internet. Most teachers allowed their students to use the computers during their class hour, permissible under the pretension that it was for school-related research. It was near the end of his math period and Adam sat in front of a screen. He'd been writing a report about sweatshops for his technical writing class. While doing some online investigating, he ran the search engine to find a famous model. He recalled she had a new line of clothing out and was checking to see if she might've pursued the use of cheap labor. Dozens of matches came up, and after noticing a hyperlink that mentioned the model being in Central America, he clicked on it.

The image on the screen was of a girl with long strands of reddish-brown hair that came down over a bare shoulder. The contours of her rich caramel-colored skin glistened, with barely a trace of her sultry bathing suit as she lay on a stone slab. The sand surrounding her appeared radiant under the light of a golden sun.

Mrs. Freud had walked in just in time to notice a pretty girl on Adam's computer screen. *There wasn't anything offensive,* Adam tried to explain, but she wouldn't hear it. She told him to log off, then go with her.

Counselor Mathis managed to speak with Adam regarding the school policy on web browsing, and the whole time, he couldn't log onto his computer because he'd forgotten his password, and so the meeting was brief.

Adam had returned to class a few minutes later, though his computer privileges in *that* class had been terminated.

Mr. Ford's voice bellowed. "I'll talk to him in a minute. Just let him take a seat for now."

Mrs. Freud's eyes were glazed over when she came back, holding her glasses in one hand and the uncapped marker she still carried in the other.

Adam expected her eyes to pop. He'd never seen her that angry before.

"You wait right there. Mr. Ford will call you in a minute." She turned and left.

Adam waited.

A few minutes had passed when he saw Mr. Ford approaching with his distinct shirt-and-tie image reserved for persons in positions worthy of respect. Mr. Ford stood watching, before he gestured for Adam to come.

Mr. Ford was a fit man in his mid-forties with short, dark brown hair and a neatly trimmed beard of the same color. Adam could see a two-way radio clipped to his back with the black antenna pressed against his shirt.

"Take a seat, Adam," he said, extending his palm out toward the seat facing his cherry-wood desk.

On the side of his desk were plaques and diplomas that formed a checkered pattern on the wall. Behind him were pictures of the school being built and various newspaper clippings.

"You want to tell me what happened?"

"I didn't mean for her to get upset. I was just asking a question."

"She said you were just trying to get everyone's attention—disrupting her class."

"I didn't mean to."

"Did you try apologizing to her?"

Adam was silent. Quite frankly, no, he hadn't tried.

"You know if you were to say something that causes hysteria, it would only be appropriate to apologize. Now, I know you're not a troublemaker, right, Adam? So let's just try and be a little more careful about the comments we make. And always get the teacher's approval first. Don't just blurt things out—raise your hand."

Adam, while agreeing that what he'd done was wrong, felt angry for being blamed, but it was an anger that dissipated quickly as he realized he was getting off easy. "Okay."

"Look, it's not like you did anything treacherous, just show some respect, that's all I ask."

Adam nodded.

"It isn't entirely your fault; she's been under a lot of stress, so she's a little vulnerable. You can hang around here until passing period, but apologize to her on Monday, okay?"

"Yes, sir," Adam offered his compliance, but shot a puzzled look at Mr. Ford. "Could I transfer to another class, Mr. Ford?"

"I'm afraid that's a requirement course; you have to take Freud."

Mr. Ford arose and leaned out of his office to tell Tina, the receptionist, that he was going to check on the air system as it was being repaired. The radio on his back crackled and someone spoke through it in hissing sounds as Mr. Ford left the office.

Adam realized he was hungry and considered eating the wrapped sandwich sitting on Mr. Ford's desk. He got up instead and went over to the waiting area, slumping his arms over the reception desk.

"Mr. Ford said I could hang around here until the bell rings."

Without looking up from her paperwork, Tina said, "Getting yourself into trouble this morning, Adam?"

"Nah, I just asked her a question—she's all uptight. I didn't have breakfast. Can I go get some chips and a soda?"

"Okay, sweetie, just don't get me in trouble. Don't go anywhere you're not supposed to, then come right back."

Adam smiled, then turned and grabbed his backpack. As he passed his Algebra classroom, the door was open again and everyone was sitting quietly.

Just beyond her door, Adam took the stairs.

The first floor was mostly reserved for the cafeteria. The walls there expanded upward the entire length of the building. Trays and dishes clattered nearby, and the cafeteria staff laughed and chatted among themselves.

Adam bought some cheese crackers and a citrus soda. He went to find a place to sit, when he noticed a fellow classmate at one of the round wooden tables sitting alone.

"What's up, Cory?"

Cory arranged his papers before looking up. "Hey, I'm working on my book report for Mr.

Wayne. I was absent the last two classes, and it's due today. He said I could work on it and present mine next week. I'll type it at home, so it's no problem."

Cory was ADHD, and without medication he couldn't control his impulsiveness and random outcries. He appeared younger than the other kids his age; he was frail, with boney arms and thin legs. His hair was a bush-like display of untamed blond curls that hung over his ears and above his eyes. He moved constantly, crossing his legs, putting his hands on one knee, exchanging legs, all while rocking in his chair.

Adam liked him, so he offered him some cheese crackers.

"Yeah, our report's due Monday. I did the visuals, but haven't come around to writing anything yet," Adam said to Cory, then asked, "Which book did you choose?"

"Sphere," Cory said with his mouth full.

"Really? Me too."

Mr. Wayne was the technical writing instructor. Earlier in the semester, he'd given his students a long list of science fiction novels to choose from and then write a report about.

"Yeah, I love Michael Crichton. You know, I've

already read several books on the list." Cory named off a few. "But most of those books are kind of old. This one's a little newer. I love it when they start setting up the bombs and—"

"No wait, don't tell me," Adam said. "I haven't finished it yet."

"Dude, you only have two days to finish the book and write about it, and it has to be typed," Cory said, and smiled.

"Three days," Adam corrected.

Cory shrugged.

"I'm at the part when the guy starts talking to the computer, spaceship, or whatever."

"That's not even halfway through the book." Cory laughed. "Good luck."

Crossing through the sea of tables, a figure started making its way closer.

"Shouldn't you be in class?" said Dave in a deep voice, then grinned, forming indentations on the sides of this thin face.

"I got kicked out," Adam replied.

Cory looked at Adam, then fumbled through his notebook papers, staring at the pages.

Dave said proudly, "I got bored in Mr. Oberman's class. I just walked out. He can't do nothing to me." He looked around, then changed his tone. "I'm going back before he sends somebody out to look for me. He probably thinks I'm in the restroom," he said, before leaving.

Adam decided to get up. "I'll see you later, Cory."

Cory rocked back and forth in his chair and gave a little wave.

Adam checked in with Tina at the office.

"It's only ten minutes until the bell. Can I leave now, Mrs. Gallegos?" Adam said, always referring to teachers and staff by their last names. "I want to get some things from my locker."

"Okay. I don't want to see you here next week. You understand, boy?"

As Adam was going down the hall, he noticed a girl at the water fountain pulling her hair over a shoulder as she bent down. A stream of water shot up and struck her in the face. Someone had placed chewing gum on the mouthpiece. Adam assumed it to be Dave's japery and couldn't help but laugh at the victim rubbing her face as she walked away.

The bell chimed and students began to flood the halls.

Adam was at his locker putting books away and sorting through the disheveled mess inside. He scavenged out a science book and a black-and-white plaid shirt, stuffing them into his backpack before shutting his locker.

Edward, Mark, John, and Anthony walked together toward Adam.

It turned out that young Benjamin, Mrs. Freud's son, had been made fun of and had started to cry, they found out after Adam left. Also, one of them explained that a flat plane could exist because it only existed in theory—Mrs. Freud found this out after asking another math teacher. Mark had made a comment after she revealed the trueness of the flat plane, 'So, it's real only that it's fake,' but quickly apologized after being given a poised stare. 'I don't want to get kicked out,' he'd said. 'I'm sorry.'

Anthony asked for his calculator back and Adam handed it to him, then watched as the troop marched down the stairs—with the exception of John, who visited his locker.

"I wish you could say stuff like that to her all the time. Why can't you say stuff like that to her all the time?" John urged.

"I wasn't even trying. It just came out."

John gave Adam's shoulder a friendly punch and, while smiling, said, "That was funny, Adam."

A light touch rested on Adam's arm. He turned

to find Valery standing there, looking concerned.

"What happened?"

"Mrs. Freud kicked me out."

"I know. I just saw Mark and Edward as I was coming up the stairs. What happened?"

"Nothing."

"So, she sent you to Mr. Ford's office for . . . ?"

"For asking her about this problem she was explaining on the board. She got all pissed, said I was disrupting her class."

Valery stared at Adam. "Is that it?"

"Yeah, really, that's what happened."

"What'd Mr. Ford say?"

"He was cool about it. Said she was under a lot of stress and I should be more polite to her. But I didn't get in trouble."

"That's all?"

"That's it."

"Mr. Ford can be cool, but I can't stand Mrs. Freud. I hate her class," Valery said. "All we do is sit there." She opened her locker and exchanged some textbooks.

John looked into his locker and said, "It feels like I'm forgetting something."

"Hey, John, let's go watch a movie?" Adam offered.

John shrugged. He took his books out of his backpack and put them back in his locker.

"Val, you want to come?" Adam asked.

"Where?"

"Me and John are going to the mall, probably watch a movie."

"But we have that test in fourth period."

"I'll take it later."

"Aw, man, but I studied and everything."

"You don't have to go, Val. We'll hang out some other time."

"I want to, but I can't."

Adam smiled. "It's cool."

"You guys be careful," she said before leaving.

Adam turned to John. "Let's go."

John slung his backpack onto his shoulders, smiling ever so unusually.

TWO

The towering structure in the center of the mall dwarfed the entrance below, hidden under a massive shadow that blanketed the parking lot before the morning sun had risen over.

Adam drove through the shaded lot and turned into an empty spot not far from the entrance.

John stepped out of the car, and stopped to look at it. "You ever thought about washing your car?"

The car's white paint appeared ashen, covered by a residual film of dirt that darkened gradually toward the bottom.

Adam got out and closed the door. Unable to remember the last time he'd washed it, he replied, "I think I washed it once, after I got it."

"That was like two years ago. If I had a car, I'd

keep it clean."

They walked along a narrow sidewalk approaching the entrance when John suddenly offered Adam some aesthetic advice. "You need a haircut."

Adam reached for the door handle and caught a glimpse of his image on the glass before it beamed away with the motion of the door.

"I don't see anything wrong with it," Adam said. He held the door open, and after John walked through, he followed.

The mall smelled of baked bread as they passed a sign that read COUNTRY KITCHEN, the words spelled out in green neon lights above a wagon wheel mounted on the wall. It was too late for breakfast and it wasn't quite lunchtime, but several persons could be seen in the booths, some wearing ordinary clothes, and others in shirts and ties.

"Look at it. It looks like you just got out of bed. You should trim it. If you got a haircut, I bet a lot more girls would talk to you, Adam."

"You know what I think?"

"What?"

"I think you just want me to look like you. You know girls want to meet guys with good-looking friends, so in reality, by saying I need a haircut, you're just looking out for yourself."

John laughed. "You're funny, Adam."

Adam meant to be serious.

John drifted off their path toward a corner shop with a psychedelic sign over the entrance, and stopped to admire a display of leather hiking boots. He reached for a bulky brown boot and inspected it from various angles, then turned it upright so he could look inside. He leaned forward, putting his nose into the shoe sole, and inhaled.

Adam watched curiously. *Is this how he shops for shoes? What's next? Will he caress the socks to his cheek?*

As they walked farther into the mall, John brought up his favorite subject: girls. "What about Audrey? I heard she likes you. Her friend Stephanie says you're her type."

The next store they stopped in had a showy display of lights that beamed from the ceiling and throughout the store were television screens with retro-images of patterns that twirled and rotated to the sound of energetic dance music. A young Indian man, dressed in black dress pants and dress shoes and a pressed shirt, approached them and asked, "Need any help, fellas?"

"We're just looking," John said, and the clerk

walked away.

"I'm her type?" Adam said, raising his voice over the sound of thudding music.

John flipped through a rack of shirts, looking them up and down before jerking each one over to one side.

"Yeah, you know. You're her type." John stopped looking through the clothes rack and added, "Girls are kind of funny, in the way they like guys. A girl might like a tall guy, or one with long hair. You've got that kind-of-buff thing going. And you're serious. You have that don't-mess-with-me look."

After they'd finished looking around, Adam followed John into the shop next door, and once inside, Adam said, "I saw Audrey the other day at lunch."

"And?"

"Nothing. I was sitting outside, on the brick wall. She was with that dark-skinned girl, you know, that girl she's always hanging around with."

John faced color-coded stacks of blue jeans folded and arranged neatly inside a large shelf made of box compartments, then turned to Adam.

"That's Stephanie," he said. "Yeah, I've got her for a class."

John moved slowly as he continued browsing

and eventually disappeared behind a partition that served as a clothes rack.

Adam stayed close to the blue jeans where he appeared to be talking to himself. "Well, they were walking by. She was eating these animal crackers, so she asked if I wanted some."

"What did you say?" John asked from behind the partition.

"I said I was a vegetarian. She gave me a weird look. I was trying to make her laugh, but she just walked away."

John poked his head around the slender display, and said, "She was trying to talk to you, Adam. You should've talked to her." He walked around and stood near Adam.

"I did talk to her."

"I mean, you should've started a conversation. Said 'yeah' and had one of those animal crackers."

Adam thought about it; he supposed she could've been trying to start a conversation with him, *but wasn't she just being nice?*

They left the store and visited another. Adam, who believed they were all pretty much the same, didn't question John's conspicuous need for comparison.

Adam and John walked past a brand-new SUV

surrounded by festive banners. To one side was the registration table with entry forms and a few scattered pens. The cardboard sign on the table read, WIN ME, and Adam thought how funny it would be to fish out one of the slips and call that person, congratulating them on winning a brand-new car.

Past the SUV was an escalator, where they went to be slowly lifted to the second level.

The little boy a few steps ahead resisted as his mother tugged on his shirt sleeve.

"You have to give me your hand, because a little boy was riding the escalator and his legs got stuck because he wouldn't give his mommy his hand," the lady said.

The boy stared at her skeptically, waiting until they reached the top before taking her hand.

Once upstairs, John was drawn toward a colorful window sign announcing a sale, 50%-75% OFF. Leaving Adam behind, he walked into the store and began rummaging through the hoards of clothing enticingly displayed on tables and clothes racks. He shuffled through the racks, then with some excitement, said, "I'm going to try on these pants," with a few pairs hanging over his forearm.

Adam pointed to a shop nearby. "I'll be over

there," he said.

The store was just beyond the crossover that connected the two sides of the second floor and Adam studied the sparkling silver letters over the entrance that read, RAPIDZ, making mental note of the letters he would want to mimic the next time they asked him to paint a banner at school, something he'd started doing this year.

Rock music played from a radio on a shelf behind two employees stationed at the counter: a bleach-blond man with a potbelly and tattoos, and a girl with pale skin and short black hair with long pink bangs that came down the sides of her face.

"Hi there," the girl said.

"Hey, how's it going, man?" the blond man welcomed Adam with a nod.

Adam examined the four walls, turning his body in a complete circle before raising one hand in a wave. "Hi," he said.

This being the only store to catch Adam's attention, he took his time examining their extravagant apparel. One particular t-shirt with anime-style drawings across the chest caught his attention, and he decided to buy it right away.

Adam placed it on the glass counter and the girl with pink hair removed the hanger.

"You like Sons of Dragons?" she asked.

"No," said Adam, "I just thought it was a cool shirt."

"That show kicks ass," she said, folding the shirt into a square with only the logo showing, then placed it neatly into a plastic bag.

Now that Adam's shopping was done, he went to the store where he'd left John, but didn't see him. He made a full circle of the area, but the surrounding shops showed no sign of his friend. Adam took a seat on one of the benches, hoping to catch him walking among the passing shoppers.

After an hour, Adam left his post to purchase a soda from the Cookie Store. On his way back, Adam still saw no sign of John. He sat on another bench this time and figured it was best to stay put. Sooner or later, his friend would have to pass by. Waiting there, he thought of the funny way he had met John, smiling as he remembered.

Two ten-year-old little boys, fourth-graders, had come out of different ends of the school building to face off on the black top of the basketball court after school.

They had liked the same girl and as a consequence of being young and relentless, neither would relinquish their preempted infatuation. The two boys stood inches away from each other, so close that Adam could smell the peanut butter on John's breath as he spoke.

"I heard you've been talking to Amanda," John had told him.

Bystanders had amassed to lay witness to the fight, and encourage it as well.

John was scrawny and boney-armed, wearing a long shirt that skirted past his waist. Enhancing his stick figure look were comically large ears sticking out through his overgrown, matted brown hair.

Adam was a whole head taller, and being a chubby kid, he'd felt confident with his advantage.

"Yeah, so what?" Adam said.

"You'd better leave her alone. She's my girl."

"She calls me on the phone. She isn't going out with you."

"Everybody knows she's my girl. Leave her alone or I'll knock you out," John said, holding a fist up to Adam's chest.

"You can't hurt me, shaggy."

"*Ooooh.*" The kids had stirred on.

"I'm not scared of you, jellybean."

The crowd of children broke out into laughter.

"You'd better stay away from her! I'm warning you, Adam! You think you're a badass. I'm not scared of you."

They stared each other down, but the spectacle posed no real threat and they eventually went their separate ways.

In the end, Amanda ended up liking someone else, but it led Adam and John to discover their other similarities, they later found out. They both enjoyed drawing and they both played soccer, and liked the same video games. They lived within walking distance of each other and became best friends in the end.

Adam waited. He didn't wear a watch and wasn't sure how long he'd been there, but was certain the same people had passed him several times. He dumped the soft drink into the trash bin and made up his mind to look for John.

On his third round through the same department store, Adam heard a woman's friendly voice and, when he looked, she was speaking to John, who preyed on her good looks.

Adam stood in the middle of an aisle, not wanting to interrupt, but hoping to catch John's attention. He watched as the girl grabbed something off the clothes rack and placed it on John's chest, holding it by the hanger. John shook his head in disagreement, though he never relieved himself of his thin smile. John's hands motioned as he spoke. Adam couldn't hear what he was saying, but in the distance, he could see the different expressions on John's face.

The woman led John to a checkout counter, where he paid. After paying, he started for the aisle where Adam was waiting.

"I've been looking all over for you," Adam said, frowning.

"What'd you think?" John motioned his head back to where he'd been standing.

"That yellow shirt was nice."

John snickered. "About the girl?"

"She's pretty, John, what can I say? Are we ready to leave?"

John was grinning as the receipt he pulled apart with both hands popped twice. Thick black ink said "Emily" and across the top was a phone number with the area code in parenthesis.

John reached into his bag to show Adam the pink-colored polo he'd bought. It looked strikingly similar to the one he had on. This one was a different brand though, John explained.

Adam asked John for the time and he replied it was 3 p.m. They had been there over four hours, and Adam had spent most of that time wandering aimlessly.

John proposed lunch, but Adam, who just wanted to leave, declined. “I’m cool,” he said.

“I got you, man, don’t worry,” John said.

At John’s discretion, they sat at one of the tables in the food court, and Adam watched him eat some fries. He anxiously wanted to leave. They would blow their cover if they weren’t back at school by 4 p.m., when John’s stepfather had planned to pick him up.

They stood up and left after John popped the last fry into his mouth.

Once on the highway, it was a short, uninterrupted drive back to the main road. Adam slowed as he took the exit, then parked in front of the school.

John grabbed his backpack from the back seat and had one foot out the door. “Hey, thanks, Adam. Sorry for disappearing for such long a time,” he said, followed by a shrug.

“It’s cool, John, no problem.”

“Cool, I’ll see you Sunday at work.”

“Yeah man, later.”

John stepped down and blended in with the crowd.

Students were coming out of the front doors,

passing Adam's car as he waited for them to clear.

Adam shifted the gear into drive and was ready to leave when he heard a pounding sound across the trunk of his car. Assuming the worst, he turned to see what happened and was surprised to see Valery standing there, looking at him through the rearview mirror.

She walked around, then leaned into the passenger window and said, "Hey, cutie."

Adam looked around before realizing she meant him. He smiled, and asked, "Do you need a ride, Val?"

"Hold on," she said, then walked over and met with another girl.

As he waited, Adam glanced down at the intertwined wires that dangled from the side of his car stereo. He'd installed it himself and couldn't reach back far enough to run the wires correctly, and because the new stereo had been smaller than the old one, a wadded paper shoved into one side kept the radio in position, but it fell out when driving over hard bumps. Adam was putting in a CD when Valery came back.

She sat in the passenger seat, placing her backpack between her feet, and fastened her seatbelt.

"I was going to catch the bus with Gracie," said Valery. Gracie was a friend who lived up the road from her. "I offered her a ride, but she said she was going to stay and type her paper. Did you guys watch a movie?"

"Nah, John went shopping."

Adam drove away and Valery went on about how unjust her teachers were and how all the homework they had assigned had ruined her weekend.

While Adam listened to most of what she had to say, he found himself feeling preoccupied with thoughts of his own. It seemed lately that Adam dreaded having to go home after school, and while he hadn't attended a full day of school today, it was still that time of day.

It was quiet now that Valery had stopped talking. Adam hadn't said anything the entire time.

"What's wrong?" she asked.

Adam didn't answer right away. He'd arrived at her house and turned the radio down before he pulled over. He looked at her in the passenger seat with her delicate hands resting in her lap, waiting for Adam's response.

"I don't know. I guess I'm just frustrated or something. I'm sorry."

"I understand. I'm beat myself." Valery raked her fingers through her dark hair, then rested her arm on the open window of the car door. "I'm ready to take a hot shower, eat something, and watch TV," she said, looking at herself in the passenger's-side mirror. She looked over at Adam. "What are you doing tonight?"

"After work, nothing."

"I'll be here if you want to call me."

Adam nodded.

"Thanks, Adam." Valery reached over and patted his shoulder. She got out and made her way up the driveway where her older brother and two friends made use of the patio furniture on the front porch.

Just a few streets and one stop sign later, Adam was home.

He heard a crunching sound as the car rolled over the gravel driveway, customary of older households before concrete driveways became the norm. The old house he'd lived in his whole life was in the worst shape he could remember, deteriorating from years of neglect. Several of the siding boards had fallen off, while the ones that remained were no longer white; instead they'd become smutty and dull and gray. The window trim had a faded blue paint that was entirely cracked, exposing the weathered wood underneath.

Adam crossed the green lawn with overgrown gangly weeds, then headed up the fractured sidewalk leading to the front steps.

Once at the house, Adam fumbled for his keys, unlocked the front door, and walked in.

Laughter roared, ensued by applause.

Adam wasn't surprised to find his mother watching television on the blue couch his father had bought his mother last year for their wedding anniversary; twenty years of fighting, reconciled by a living room set.

"Hey, Mom." Adam locked the door behind him.

Adam's mother faced the television and with her head tilted upward, her puckered lips released a slather of gray smoke.

"Hi," she said, once the smoke had come out. She crushed the white cigarette butt with her fingertips. The nearby ceramic ashtray with a row of grooves along the center was engrossed with contorted, white stems.

Adam walked through the living room, and routinely glanced at the framed picture of a single flower they owned since he could remember. On a nearby table, a picture of Adam's parents showed them cutting their cake on their wedding day. The wall near a glass table displayed a Christmas picture of Adam and his sister from when they were small; Adam was in a large box, wrapped like a present, and his sister pretended to open the gift.

The room closest to the entrance was his parents', and near the dining room was his sister's.

The back of the cozy two-bedroom house had a den which had become Adam's room once he became too big to share one. It was warm and the air was stagnant, and as he went inside, he pulled the curtain back and opened a window. Adam flung the backpack off his shoulder and it landed on his old wooden office chair. Stacked beside his monitor were his American History, Physics, and Spanish III textbooks, which sat on a white metal desk with filing drawers on one side. There were no electrical sockets in the den and a small cutout in the wall led an orange extension cord from his sister's room to Adam's, where a computer, a small radio, and a lamp were plugged to the multi-connector behind his desk. He took the plaid shirt out of his backpack and watched it land on the hand-me-down queen-sized bed with wire springs that would pop and cause soreness if he slept for too long.

Adam put a hand over his empty stomach, then went to the kitchen and peeked into the fridge. Those cheese crackers were the last thing he'd eaten. There was nothing already made; nothing he could've just thrown into the microwave. He glanced at the time on the microwave clock. It was 4:30, and he should've been at work by now. Running late as usual, he settled for a handful of chips.

Music blared from Victoria's room as she opened her door. It was a mess inside, her clothes strewn over cluttered furniture. The walls of her room were wallpapered in teenaged heartthrob posters.

Adam purposefully altered their names, knowing it would throw Victoria into a tantrum. The only thing to make her madder was teasing her that she had a different father, as she looked nothing like Adam, with hazel-colored eyes and golden brown hair.

She wore a pair of small denim shorts and an orange t-shirt. Her sandals flopped on the hardwood floor as she trudged into the living room.

"I need twenty dollars for my science fair project. It's due Monday, and if I don't turn one in, I'll fail," Adam heard her say, as he stood in the kitchen.

"You'll have to wait until your father comes home, Vicky. I don't have any money."

Adam dusted his hands. He went to the living room, reached into his wallet, and gave his sister the money she needed.

Victoria ran off, grabbed the cordless phone, and rapidly skimmed the dial pad.

One last thing before leaving, Adam needed to use the restroom; he'd been holding it since they left the mall. He washed his face and found a bottle of rubbing alcohol to clean a pimple that had appeared on his chin. When he saw the toilet paper roll sitting on the bathroom floor beside the toilet, he became irate. Victoria always took the rolls off the dispenser and left them on the floor. Adam finished up, placing the soap on the dish and the alcohol in the cabinet beneath the sink and the toilet paper on its coil.

Adam came out of the restroom. He stared at his mother, but she paid him no attention.

"Mom, tell Vicky to stop leaving the toilet paper on the floor."

"You already told me!" Victoria shouted from her room.

"But you don't do it!" Adam shouted back.

Victoria walked past them, placed the phone on

its charger, and cried, "Ugh. I hate this house. You think you're the boss because Mom does everything you say." The door slammed after she stormed into her room.

Adam went back to his room to get ready. His uniform consisted of a dark blue polo tucked into beige khakis, and a nametag. He wore none of that. Adam simply pulled a white smock from a hanger in his stand-alone closet and wore it over his t-shirt.

He grabbed his keys and before leaving asked his mother if she needed money.

Staring blankly at the television, she shook her head. Adam handed her ten dollars. She shoved the bill into the front pocket of her denim skirt, then placed a menthol into her mouth and lit it.

Adam left.

THREE

Parking was a nuisance at the small shopping strip La Villa. The majority of its business was due to the Hispanic-themed supermarket amid a row of stores, leaving few parking spaces vacant. Left of the supermarket was a bingo hall and on the right, the drugstore. Across the parking lot, an auto-parts store, a beauty salon, and a Chinese restaurant stood in tandem.

Adam found a parking space on the disused side of the drugstore. He rolled up both windows and locked the doors.

Billows of dark clouds loomed overhead, threatening the afternoon as he walked toward the entrance of the drugstore.

Inside, he passed through the gift card aisle,

heading toward the back where the manager's office and employee lounge joined. Blocky green letters read, ENTER PIN on the screen of the small red box that was the shift-clock mounted on the wall outside of the manager's office. He punched in his social security number, followed by the green button, and the name ADAM GARCIA appeared.

"You're twenty minutes late."

Standing behind Adam was Glen, the store manager.

Glen was tall, but had a stooped walk. He appeared shabby all the time, with strands of brown hair that dangled freely above his glasses and flared over his ears. His snug dress shirt was crookedly tucked into his pants with a wrinkled fold that stuck out behind a relaxed tie.

Adam turned to face him. "Yeah, and I'm also you're only technician."

Glen held an open tube of tennis balls, minus one, and a toy doll in a torn open box. He leaned into his office and dropped them into a shopping basket marked, DAMAGED GOODS.

Glen caught up to Adam, following him to the pharmacy. "Hey man, could you take this person on line six? She's been holding for a while." Glen smiled, revealing long, yellow-stained teeth. "I can't help her," he added.

Before Adam could reply, a voice came on the store speaker system. "I need a void on four."

Sighing with defeat, Glen dropped his head into his hands and mumbled to himself. Taking a step forward, then backward, he groped his pockets before he strode to the front of the store.

Adam pushed the waist-high swinging door leading into the pharmacy.

"There you are. I was going to have the manager call your home, see if you were coming," the pharmacist said in his Nigerian accent.

"I'm sorry, Henry. I got held up at school." Adam couldn't think of a better excuse.

Henry was smoothing out a label on an amber-colored vial. He folded the instructions and dropped the small vial into a white paper bag, then attached the instructions folio and sealed the bag with a staple.

Adam picked up the phone and pressed the button where the call was parked, indicated by a blinking red light.

"This is Adam in the pharmacy. How can I help you?"

"Finally! I've been on hold for fifteen minutes now. I need a refill."

Adam held the phone with his shoulder and counted pills as he listened. He finished his count, closed the counting tray adeptly tilting it and allowing the pills to slide into the small vial. He snapped the white lid onto the vial with a twist, then dropped it into a colored basket and pushed it across the counter.

"Okay, let me just pull up your record." While on the computer, Adam listened as the elderly woman complained.

"I've been waiting and waiting. I thought I was never going to get through."

"Okay, what's your name?"

"Jane," she said, then pronounced her last name, "Wil-son."

"Is that on Maple Road?" Adam asked, searching through names on the monitor.

"Nooo. Jane D. Wilson."

Adam found her. She had three prescriptions; two had recently been filled and one was expired.

"Is that for your antibiotics?"

"Yes, I'm out. I need a refill."

"Ma'am, you don't have any more refills on it. I'm going to have to call the doctor. If he okays it, we can call you when it's ready, most likely tomorrow," Adam explained.

"Well, my doctor said I had three refills."

"I'm sorry, but it only had two. We can call and ask him if you need any more."

She went silent.

Adam could hear a television set in the background over the pharmacy noise. He continued to count more pills as Henry whispered that customers were waiting.

"You said you'll call me tomorrow," she said, finally.

"We have to get a hold of the doctor first. I don't know if he'll be in tomorrow."

"Okay, fine."

"Thank you," Adam said before hanging up. He bottled more pills and handed Henry the basket.

Adam printed Mrs. Wilson's label and filed it into the call-in box after writing the word *Refill* on the top margin.

There was nothing too demanding about the job other than the tedious verification of each bottle's control number, a ten-digit code that assured the validity of the drug. Obligated by law, the pharmacist always checked it before labeling the drug, unerringly; only he could carry out the labeling process.

Adam took one of the small plastic baskets from

the high stack that served as a queue, with a prescription inside each one waiting to be filled. With the basket in hand, he retrieved the medication from one of the metal shelves behind the counter, and counted the pills. He printed the label and instructions and placed it back into the basket, ready for the pharmacist to review.

"Hey, is my prescription ready yet?"

Adam couldn't see the tall man's face under his green billed cap. He held a reflective vest in his hands, standing at one of the unmanned registers.

Henry turned toward the man, pointing a finger at him. "What was your name again?"

"Duncan."

"Last name?"

"Moore," the man said. "Duncan Moore."

"Did you already print it?" Adam asked as he began to go through the stacks of baskets.

"Yes." Henry pointed in Adam's direction. "It should be in there."

Adam took the basket, then went back to where the medication was, only to find an empty space on the shelf.

"We're out of Pro Packs." Adam handed Henry the basket.

Henry walked back, glanced at the top shelf, then

told the customer, "Sir, I'm sorry, we're out of the Pro Pack. I can call to check if another pharmacy has it."

"I can't believe this! I've been waiting for an hour! *You* said it'd be ready in an hour, and *now* you tell me you don't got it!"

"I apologize. I am in lack of assistance and I didn't look to see."

"Give me my prescription back!" He held an arm over the counter while his fingers beckoned.

Henry dug through the baskets and handed the man his prescription.

The tall man stomped off. "Geez, where's the manager?"

Henry asked Adam to delete the man's information from the computer, then he took the printed label and tore it into pieces, throwing it away.

Tiffany, the cashier that worked in the pharmacy was a sunny-faced blonde with sultry hips. She walked behind the counter where Adam counted pills.

"It's been like this all day," she said.

"Has it?" said Adam.

Tiffany reached with both hands and with her head tilted, her fingers raked through her long golden hair. She removed a hair band from her wrist before twisting her hair together into a bun.

A customer approached the counter and Tiffany went back to the register where she logged in.

Greeting Tiffany with a friendly smile was a black woman in her thirties wearing a dark pantsuit that complemented her figure nicely. She reached into her purse and asked for Wallace.

Plastic slots were organized in alphabetical order on the gray metal shelves behind the cashier. Tiffany held the W-Z file and looked through the packets.

"Lamar?" she asked with the container resting on her hip.

"Yes, that's it. That's my granddad." The woman paid, and her heels tapped sharply in rhythmic steps as she left.

Since Adam began been working at the pharmacy, he learned to familiarize himself with the commoners. He knew who had diabetes, who had high blood pressure, who was on birth control, and he could unmistakably recognize the atrophic heroin addicts who would come in on occasion trying to buy syringes.

Adam thought about the day he applied for the job. He'd sat nervously in one of the plastic seats in the waiting area of the pharmacy, rubbing his clammy palms on his brown corduroy pants, awaiting his interview. After each wipe, he rubbed his hands together and felt the calloused blisters he'd gotten from working construction with his dad the entire summer. There hadn't been an ad, or a webpage where he could apply; he simply walked in the store and asked if he could have a job. The manager asked him a couple of questions. How old are you? Do you go to school? In response to Adam's answers, the manager quickly announced that they were accepting applications for part-time positions. The manager had gone to fetch an application while Adam, who had walked several blocks from the bus stop, took a seat.

The pharmacist at the time was a younger man, mirthful and easygoing. He wasn't wearing a smock, now that Adam thought of it. The pharmacist had peeked over one of the registers and asked, "Hey. You waiting on a prescription?"

"No," Adam said, "I'm waiting on Cole." The manager had said to call him by his first name.

"You are?" The pharmacist smiled and adjusted his glasses. "Why don't you come here for a second?" He motioned a hand in a limp flop.

Adam had approached the counter but the

pharmacist motioned for him to come around.

"You ever work in a pharmacy before?" He'd been chewing a piece of gum as he spoke.

"No," Adam admitted.

"Would you like to learn?"

Adam looked at the technicians, keying orders on the computer, counting pills, and putting medication back on the shelves.

"I'm going to the new grocery store they just built right down the road. And I'm taking my technicians with me, so I need someone to learn this stuff. Think you can manage?"

"Yes," Adam assured him.

"Can you start today?"

Adam hadn't planned on it, but if it meant getting a job, he said, "Yeah."

"Great."

The pharmacist gave Adam a basic tour of all the happenings and responsibilities at the pharmacy. The closet in the back had extra supplies. Beyond that, there was a sink and a refrigerator. The pharmacist described the order in which the medication was arranged, but mentioned that it would come naturally as Adam acquainted himself better. He stressed the importance of checking the medication and stopped to show Adam how they were counted, by fives. He showed Adam how to use the automated machine. The gray box mounted on the wall held some of the more commonly used drugs and counted the pills as they flowed into a vial. Last, he went over the fundamentals of the computer system.

The pharmacist also mentioned that Adam only had five days to learn everything. The most complicated part, it seemed to Adam, was learning to read the doctor's handwritten inscriptions. Surprisingly, a few days later Adam was working completely on his own.

The rest of the night was fast-paced which helped the time pass with ease. The pharmacy stopped taking in prescriptions at 8 p.m., and the last hour for pick-ups was at 9 p.m. when the pharmacy closed.

The weekend wasn't as hectic; John and Anthony had obtained part-time jobs in the pharmacy, but neither could work school nights.

Adam shelved the medications and filed the hardcopy prescriptions, then placed a dozen or so labels in the call-in box for approval, but some of them wouldn't get approved until Monday.

Adam's last order of business was to scan the barcodes of the low-stock drugs and use the

handheld device to send the order through a phone's receiver in a series of fax-like bleeps.

By 9:30 p.m., the drugstore was deserted. Adam was beat and his legs were sore and his eyes had formed dark circles.

Tiffany hung her smock on a clothing hook in the supply closet. She went over to Adam and let out a moan of relief as she stretched. "I didn't feel like coming in today, but then I remembered it was Friday."

As the pharmacy closed, Tiffany was allowed to leave. Henry thanked her and said goodbye.

"Goodbye," she said.

"Bye," said Adam from behind the counter.

Minutes later, Glen appeared. He hung his arms over the pharmacy wall slothfully. He looked at Adam and said, "Hey, want to face?"

Adam was sitting on a wooden stool drinking a Coke Henry had bought him. Without saying a word, Adam shook his head.

Glen walked off.

It was the cashier's duty to face the store at night, push all the products forward—a standard retail procedure to persuade customers to spend more somehow.

Instead, Adam walked through the store to do

some shopping. Trying to remember everything he needed, he picked up a can of shaving cream, a deodorant, and soap. Glen was sitting in his office when Adam asked him to ring up the products.

"I can't," Glen said. "I already collected the money from the registers."

Adam nodded in understanding as Glen scribbled something down on the backside of a torn sheet of paper, then pushed it aside on his desk. Glen then reached over to a stack of envelopes and handed Adam his paycheck.

Adam took the check, placing it in his pocket, then put the toiletries down on Glen's desk and clocked out. Adam said goodnight to Henry who was stapling prescriptions in the dark as he passed him on his way out the door.

It had started raining, and fat droplets of water were plummeting from the awning, splattering into the little stream of water that had formed on the sidewalk. Rain slivers twinkled in the headlights of a remaining vehicle in the empty lot.

Adam pulled his smock over his head and dashed toward his car. He unlocked the door, adjusted himself, and turned the key in the ignition.

The car didn't start.

He looked around for the pair of pliers he kept on the floor of the car. They were deep under the passenger's seat, along with a penny, a wadded receipt, and some gooey stuff he wished he hadn't touched.

The rain drummed on the hood of the car as Adam pulled the lever that would release it.

Under the hood, the battery terminals were encrusted in heaping piles of white oxidation. Adam tapped on them with the pliers, then closed the hood. The second time, the car started.

FOUR

The lock snapped loudly on the front door as Adam entered the darkness of his house. His mother had gone to bed and the door to Victoria's room was open, meaning she wasn't home and the only sound was that of Adam's squeaky shoes as he walked.

He kicked his shoes off on the aged laminate floor in his room and collapsed onto the bed. The springs creaked and the headboard tapped against the wall as Adam's body settled. He closed his eyes and felt everything around him melt away, the pitter-patter of rain lolling him to sleep.

The sound of a gurgling engine grew louder as it pulled into the driveway.

Adam awakened, and as the engine cut off, he

was left wondering whether to stay in bed or help his drunken father out of his truck.

The night before, Adam had made a trip to the garbage can when he noticed his father's blue Chevrolet sitting outside. He could see a figure through the back window of the truck's cab. Looking inside, Adam had found his father sitting on the passenger's side of his truck, asleep. No one was behind the wheel. Just a sole, bearded man, with his head slumped over, one arm resting on the back of the seat, and a crumpled package of cigarettes clinched in his fist.

A piercing metallic sound had emanated from the door as Adam pulled it back and looked at the representation of his future self. He joggled his father, who woke up startled with blood-shot eyes that searched the inside of the cab. It took a few minutes, but Adam finally helped him slide off the seat, then he helped his father to the front door, regulating his balance. During the short walk, Adam could hear his father's t-shirt flapping in the breeze.

Adam found it astonishing—his father always managed to make it home in one piece, as if alcoholics were programmed with a form of autopilot, finding their way home from wherever they practiced their ritual.

There was little Adam could do for his father. Degrading as it was, the children of this incessant alcoholic grew up knowing two things: that Dad had a problem, and not to talk about the problem with anyone. Adam's father was completely ascetic to his grim substance abuse; albeit he would stop for a few days, he became a baleful walking time-bomb ready to go off at something he claimed to have suddenly found irritable. Common practice was, with tolerance from his family, he could go on that way for about a week, but eventually he'd revert to drinking.

A knock battered on the door.

Adam sprung out of bed. He unzipped his smock, letting it go somewhere in the dark, then stopped to adjust his dangling socks. As he passed through the dark house disoriented, he found the front door guiding himself with the faint light that shown through the living room windows from the street lamp outside. Adam opened the door.

His father stood there, with a beet-red face and a dazed look in his eyes. The odor coming from him wafted with the sour stench of alcohol as he mumbled a few incoherent slurs.

Adam couldn't help but notice his father's

unzipped fly as he came in, shifting his body to each side before taking a step.

Adam's father, Ramon, shambled to the coffee table in the middle of the living room, bumping into it. He stopped, shrugged his shoulders as if telling it he didn't know, then walked around it.

Adam stood watching him, then closed and locked the door. He sneaked past him to avoid making contact and was halfway through the kitchen when the light came on.

From behind, he heard his father say, "Hungry! Wa di-u mate, ta eat"—or so it sounded.

Ramon turned away, taking uneven steps that thumped sluggishly through the dining room. He pulled back a wooden chair and it tattered against the floor, reverberating through the quiet house, then plopped down at the table.

Adam opened the fridge and looked around. An open pack of American singles hid behind a half-empty gallon of milk. The middle shelf fit smaller objects. It had a carton of eggs, a tub of butter, and some salsa. Two store-brand sodas, some grape jam, and a jar of mayonnaise were the only things on the door. On the lowest shelf was a pan of refried beans no one seemed to have been particularly fond of. Adam grabbed the pan along with a half-eaten bowl of rice he'd found behind the beans. He scraped up a few spoonfuls of beans, put it in with the rice, and nuked it.

As the food turned, Adam leaned against the countertop rubbing his eyes with his palms.

The kitchen had been remodeled a few years back, only it still appeared old-fashioned. The mustard-yellow gas stove was on the same side as the matching refrigerator. The ceiling was soiled and darkened with grease spots—some as large as cup saucers—from the constant frying and lack of ventilation.

The microwave sounded.

Adam grabbed a fork, then took the steaming bowl over to the dining table where he pushed aside the encrusted dirty plate from the night before as his father was wont to sit in the same spot.

Adam went back to the fridge and brought out a Tupperware of his mother's salsa. He plopped a spoon into that and set it down on the table.

Just as he put everything away, Adam heard his father yell out, "Tortillas!"

Of course, how could Adam have been so inconsiderate? The tortillas; this man couldn't eat without them.

In the junk drawer, Adam rummaged through the clutter in search of a lighter. At the stove, he turned on the burner, then placed the square griddle on the metal grate. He reached into the fridge where he brought out some tortillas, undid the twist-tie, and slapped a few onto the griddle's warm surface.

Adam didn't mind tending to his father, not on nights like tonight. At least it kept his parents from fighting. Standing in the kitchen now, he was overcome by a sense of failure; destined to flip tortillas for a father who couldn't control his drinking.

The bowl Adam had placed down for his father was now doused in green salsa. Adam placed the tortillas in a folded dishcloth, the way he'd seen his mother do several times before, and set them down next to the ceramic avocado-shaped saltshaker.

He placed a few more tortillas onto the griddle, then poured a glass of water and made his father some instant tea.

While Adam waited for the second batch of tortillas to heat up, he tore a paper towel from the roll and wiped some spilled beans and a few rice grains off the countertop into his hand, then threw the wadded mess into the trash.

The only time Adam's father ever spoke was when he was drunk. He grunted something and told Adam to have a seat.

Adam, for the time being, could give him back some of his lost sense of superiority. Respectfully, he sat and listened.

Ramon tore one of the tortillas and scooped his food onto it.

"Ju' comurmur, hm?"

Adam could see the jumble of food being masticated as his father spoke. A trickle of beans had dribbled down the side of his mouth which was now meshed into his beard.

Ramon grabbed the foremost tortilla from the stack in front of him, then took a bite of food and stared at Adam from across the table.

"Wenjur term ateen, ju'help yer mom. Eh?"

The last few words were comprehensible. Adam stared beyond, nodding meagerly.

At the young age of fourteen, Ramon had left his home in Mexico, moved to the United States, and started remodeling homes. He'd been independent since and held Adam accountable to become a successful struggler like himself. He started taking Adam to work when he was just a boy, during the summer. The long hours of hard labor under the broiling Texas sun made Adam more appreciative and responsible.

"Ju' tink differend. Na me," Ramon said, pointing a bean-stained finger at Adam.

Ramon was referring to the fact that Adam had abandoned the idea of following in his father's footsteps. Now that Adam had an afterschool job, he wouldn't be joining Ramon on jobsites anymore. Ramon probably didn't mean what he said next; after all, he was impaired.

"Why onju ja leave? Eh?"

Adam drew his head back, stifling tears. He couldn't believe it; he wanted to cry. Adam got out of his chair and headed for the kitchen before his eyes could begin to water.

He put the tortillas back in the fridge, and now everything had been put away. The stove knob clicked as Adam turned it shut. He flicked off the light switch and sighed under his breath.

Adam sunk his head as he walked past his father.

Alone in his room, Adam felt a surge of anger posses him. He loathed being reproached by his drunken father. He stood in the dark looking around and could hear his breaths being drawn in through his nostrils. His chest heaved up and down with each long pull. He stopped and jerked his head toward the door when he heard the chair scrape against the floor, which meant his father had gotten up. He stood there with clutched fists, listening to his father's steps. Adam didn't notice right away that he'd been holding his breath, after hearing the chair.

Adam let go.

A long moment passed and the whole time he felt paralyzed in the dark.

It was quiet enough. Only the drops of water outside could be heard trickling from the roof.

Adam decided to turn on the lamp, and in the poorly lit room he went over and opened the top drawer of his dresser. On the floor, sitting by the bed, was his backpack. He reached for it, then went back to the dresser drawer, where a pair of boxer shorts went into the backpack, followed by a pair of socks. Adam picked out two t-shirts from the following drawer and shoved them to the bottom of his backpack.

He bent down and opened the drawer second to the bottom. Folded in half were three twenty-dollar bills Adam kept hidden under his shorts. He counted the money, an ingrained habit, then stuffed the bills into his pants pocket. Reaching over, he felt his check jutting out from his back pocket, so he pulled it out, folded it, and placed it back where it'd been, letting it sink down. After a few tumbling folds, a pair of blue jeans and his favorite plaid shirt were the last things to go into his bag before he zipped up.

Adam put on his shoes and looked around one last time, trying to remember if he needed anything else. He slung his backpack over his shoulders, adjusting the straps for a comfortable fit, then turned off the lamp. In the still and dark room, Adam gazed outside to see that it had stopped raining.

The doorknob jiggled as Adam exited the room.

There was darkness throughout the house. As Adam passed the microwave clock, he could see the sharp green numbers; it was 11:04 p.m. *Still early,* he thought.

Adam's father lay asleep on the couch with his head hobbled over the armrest, snoring loud enough to distort the nature show on television.

The Boa Constrictor can eat prey many times its size. Their jaws are lined with small, hooked teeth, perfect for grabbing on and holding to its prey while it wraps its strong body around its victim until it suffocates.

The snake on TV was moving inches away from

indigenous children sleeping on cots as the narrator claimed that it would 'not harm humans.'

Adam pulled the lock back slowly, stepped out, and locked it again with the same frailty.

FIVE

This wasn't the first time Adam found himself pursing impunity from his father. Sneaking out before, he would manage to open the door to his father's truck and put the shifter into neutral. He'd push the truck back enough so he could squeeze his own car out, maneuvering around the truck and out the driveway.

Adam unlocked the passenger door of his car, then reached inside and unlocked the back door. The plastic bag from Rapidz rustled in the dark as he pulled out the t-shirt he'd bought and stuffed it into his backpack.

While his natural inclination was to drive, he obliterated the thought. For months, since having a car, he hadn't walked anywhere. Tonight, the serenity of walking appealed to him as a way to become lost in thought. Adam locked the doors, gently pushing them shut, and afterwards, he shot a glance at his parents' windows to make sure he wasn't being watched. Quietly, he crossed the lawn, and didn't make a sound until his shoes crunched gravel as he traversed the driveway.

Adam's mom had complained a hundred times about the house in the middle of their street, and how it had 'ruined the neighborhood.' It sat empty for years and, while it was now being occupied, it lacked upkeep. Adam had only seen one of the residents, a lady tending to her overgrown shrubs which bore flowers that seemed to attract too many bees in the summer. The shrubs, however, were mitigated by the accumulation of children's toys strewn across the dirt-patched lawn.

Adam decided to go see his girlfriend, Michelle—after all, she'd still be awake. Had he not decided to leave, he would've probably called her anyway. The nights they'd talk, she'd spend most of their time on the phone telling Adam how much she missed him, how much she wanted him, and teased him playfully to come over.

They didn't see each other much, as she attended

an 'alternative' high school. Soon after Adam met her, she'd dropped out, but he convinced her to go back to school.

Adam had stood on the front porch one day after school with his friends, Robert and Jared.

Jared had met a new girl who he'd spoken with a couple times on the phone, and that night they'd arranged to meet at Jared's house.

Adam had just happened to show up and Robert filled him in.

Michelle, who was riding in the car, was the first to step out.

The guys noticed her right away. She had dark, curly hair pulled back exposing her neck, and she wore tight blue jeans that stretched like elastic over her voluptuous posterior.

"Daaamn," Jared said when he saw her.

Adam knew *that* woman wasn't Jared's mystery date; *that* girl obviously had no problems attracting the opposite sex, ergo eliminating the need to be set up with Jared.

Jared was a nice guy; he just wasn't conscious about his appearance, and the girls he'd tried to date were often repelled by his sloven attire.

After watching her for a few meaningful seconds, Adam knew he wanted her. Although he'd never had a real girlfriend before, he'd attempt to make her that person.

The girls had ridden in a two-door sports car and Michelle had gotten out to push her seat forward; that's when Jared's mystery date had been revealed.

Robert said, "Jared, that's Angelica."

"Damn." Jared grimaced.

The girl came out of the car, and to Jared's disappointment she outweighed him by a hundred pounds. She'd leave there with nothing more than an acclaimed friendship—her hopes for romance abolished, misled by a guy who spoke so kindly to her, just a few days prior.

Not wanting to be present during the girl's dejection, Adam said, "I'll leave you two alone." He smiled at Jared as he walked away toward the little sports-car Michelle sat in.

Adam introduced himself to Michelle, and being she was a year older, he lied about his age. They talked for a short while, and before she left, they exchanged phone numbers. A few months later he lost his virginity to her under the stars in an open field after attending her homecoming dance.

Anxiously, he yearned to be with her, and imagined how she would sneak him inside her house, then take him into her bedroom where she would kiss away his sorrow. They'd make love quietly so her parents wouldn't hear, and tomorrow would be a glorious, brand new day.

Orange streetlamps marked the corners of the sidewalk as Adam continued walking. The wind picked up, but the temperature remained pleasant despite it being misty.

As Adam continued, a volley of barking exploded from behind a chain-link fence. The deafening barks echoed in the distance, alerting the network of dogs throughout the neighborhood.

Adam could see the beams of a vehicle's headlamps approaching from behind. There had been few cars on the road that night and he hadn't paid much attention to this one, until it started slowing down.

Adam turned his head.

The light-colored sedan had all its windows down and rap music blared from inside.

Adam had been robbed at gun-point once before and he knew not to panic in such situations, because it only fuels those people who are trying to induce fear into their victims.

The radio was turned down and the guy in the passenger seat was now hanging halfway out the window. The car stopped and a bottle clinked as it bounced off the curb.

Adam heard one of them say, "You going to throw up or what?" ensued by laughter.

"Nah, I'm cool."

Under the assumption that he hadn't been noticed, Adam continued walking. A few paces later, he heard someone in the car say, "Hey, let's get some tacos."

The car shifted into drive and hummed as they sped off. A yellow turn-light flickered in the darkness when they turned.

Michelle lived on the side of town where the houses blended in with several stores, unlike Adam's house, where the area was mostly residential. From where he walked, he could see the store signs and the traffic of the main street ahead.

The main road was full of craters, now turned murky puddles onto which the traffic lights reflected.

Adam walked past the colorfully lit convenience store where a car drove into the parking lot.

Farther on was a restaurant across from Michelle's street. Near the entrance was a statue of a brown bear in a green Park Ranger hat, holding something in his hands, possibly a rolling pin. Adam made his way along the multilane street. Once he'd reach the bear, he'd be home-free.

Even though Adam had only gone about four miles, he'd become tired. The more he blinked, the drowsier he felt, but it didn't bother him. The only thing on his mind was Michelle.

Michelle's father did a good job of keeping the house nice. The yard was cut and the siding looked brand-new, and seeing it gave Adam a warm feeling inside.

Adam stepped up to the small, concrete porch. The moment he knocked, she answered, staring at him from behind the glass of the aluminum storm door.

Michelle didn't say anything. She didn't greet Adam as he'd expected.

Although he hadn't called, Adam didn't think she'd be too surprised; he'd knock, and after knocking she'd answer the door saying, 'Why do you have to knock so loud?' like always.

Back when they first started dating, Michelle would pick Adam up from school. Everyone knew Adam's girlfriend: the older girl with the hourglass figure and long, dark curly hair. Waiting outside of her car, she'd greet him with a hug and kiss him in the open, ensuring that anyone who looked knew the person picking up Adam was more than just his after-school ride.

Michelle opened the storm door and stared at Adam for a moment before finally asking, "What are you doing here?"

He brushed his damp hair with his fingers. The backpack seemed heavy and Adam hooked his thumbs into the straps, and let it fall to one side. He looked at the backpack on the floor, then up at her.

"I wanted to see you."

Adam thought she looked exceptionally pretty with her hair pulled back loosely in a ponytail, leaving a few curly strands of hair on each side of her face.

Michelle wore a green and white-striped football jersey cut just above her navel, with gray warm-up pants and house slippers.

"Why haven't you called me, Adam?" she said, sounding irked.

In truth, Adam wasn't a phone enthusiast. It had been three days, he guessed, since their last conversation. Telling by her stare, it hadn't been soon enough.

All the times Adam had made her upset, he'd never seen her act this way. This was serious.

Michelle had plenty of reasons to break up with Adam, and though he'd never find out which reason she chose, he could tell she already had the next man in mind.

The 'next man' was sitting on the couch watching television.

All Adam could see was the back of a shaved head contrasting against the lively images of the television set.

Adam felt his arms rise to push her out of the way, grab that lecher by the buttons of his collar shirt, and slam him into the television—which he seemed to be more interested in than *his* girlfriend.

Instead, he looked back at Michelle, and sighed.

She isn't worth it, he thought.

The scenario would be: hurt the guy, encounter police, spend the night in jail, and have to explain what happened to his parents, or leave them be and just live with it.

Painful emotions stabbed Adam like a spear through his stomach. He didn't know whether to cry or to be angry. Would he faint right there on her porch and ruin their date?

"What are you doing?" Adam asked her.

The guy looked back, assuming nothing; he couldn't see Adam standing outside. He turned his attention back to the television, drawing a can to his lips.

Michelle stepped outside and closed the door behind her.

They stood silent under the porch light, avoiding eye contact and listening to the sound of cars zoom past on the main street nearby.

The woman he'd come to love but failed to keep had now betrayed him like a hapless fool.

"I loved you, Michelle," Adam said, and waited until he had her attention. "You bitch!"

She gasped. Michelle's face turned angry, and her hands then straddled her hips.

"Who *you* calling a *bitch*?"

Funny how that seems to be the only thing a woman can say when being called the B-word.

"You asshole!" she protested.

Adam raised his eyebrows in wonderment. There wasn't much he'd do to try and stay with her. He had tried—he treated her the best way he knew how. Sure, he wasn't always there, but at least he was honest. And now it was over.

"I heard you've been going around with all these girls at school!" Michelle screamed at him.

Adam wasn't in the mood for arguing, but he pried further. "Says who?" Adam said, fully aware that she didn't know anyone else at his school but him.

"A friend."

They stood silently, until she went into a rage. "You don't call! I never know where you are, or what you're up to. Like right now!" Her eyes scanned the street. "Where's your car?"

"I walked."

"You walked? See, I can't have a boyfriend that walks over here!"

Adam picked up his backpack and went down the stairs.

As he reached the sidewalk, he noticed the shiny new muscle car he'd neglected to see earlier, it looked like something the 'next man' might drive.

"Don't you walk away from me!"

Adam looked back and noticed her hands had cupped her mouth, though she quickly removed them when she noticed him watching. The last thing he heard was the door slam as he walked farther down the sidewalk. Adam didn't even turn to look at the car that skidded to a halt and then honked as he carelessly crossed the main street.

The sky appeared a reddish color when Adam looked up.

As he walked down the street he examined the

tarred gum spots on the sidewalk, visible under the row of streetlamps. Staring at the ground, his eyes began to well up with tears, overwhelmed by the belief that she no longer loved him, and that what they had wasn't so special after all. Adam dabbed at the corners of his eyes with his shirt tail, then stopped. It felt like something erupted inside when his fist slammed onto the front of a newspaper stand. The bang was followed by a rattling sound from the chain securing it to the wooden light post.

Why?

A short time ago, Adam assured her that nothing would ever change how he felt about her, but now, he'd become unforgiving.

One day, you'll find another girl. One who'll be prettier, Adam thought, but he couldn't help feeling sorry for himself.

From where he stood, Adam could see the ornate lights of the convenience store, so he headed that way.

SIX

Adam crossed the parking lot to the convenience store where green neon lights outlined the top of the building. It was a small place that remained busy, with regular customers that walked in and out at all hours of the night.

Adam went in, catching a glimpse of his figure on the black and white security monitor located behind the clerk. He was familiar with the store, purchasing condoms a few times before at odd hours of the night. The same guy was always there, a slim man with dark hair and a mustache who revealed wire braces as he spoke.

"Hello, my friend."

"Let me get a pack of Reds," Adam said.

Adam, who didn't smoke, now felt the urge to

light up a cigarette. Several displays sat on the counter; everything from pocket knives, toys, and lighters were crammed together to one side. Adam tossed a cheap lighter onto the counter before reaching into his pocket.

"$6.47," said the clerk.

The total served as a reminder of why Adam hadn't tried them in the first place. He laid a folded twenty next to the register and heard the drawer slide out before receiving the cigarettes and his change.

Adam walked away and patted the sealed pack on his palm, not knowing the reason behind such action, other than not wanting to appear like an amateur, but no one watched him.

He looked up at the camera mounted above the doors as he pushed one open.

Adam passed the gas pumps and headed toward the main street. He spotted a payphone on the other side and waited at the edge of the parking lot for the street to clear.

It was quiet except for the sound of the payphone as it swallowed Adam's quarters in a progression of metallic gulps. Adam didn't have a cell phone. Not one that worked, anyway. His father had given him one—an old model covered in dried cement and paint stains, but it was always without service, so it sat somewhere in his room, along with a list of his contacts programmed into it. Adam stared at the silver buttons on the dial before he entered a phone number he thought would work. It rang, and as he waited, he tried to make sense of the scribbles of vandalism on the booth's enclosure.

"Ya? *Hello?*"

Adam wished it was Michelle's voice on the other end, realized Doug was on the phone, and said, "Hey, Doug."

"ADAM!" Doug said, full of excitement. "Where you calling me from, dude? I was going to let it go to voicemail."

"Where are you?" Adam asked.

"I'm outside the liquor store. Where you at?"

"I'm by Michelle's. Do you mind picking me up?"

Doug chuckled. "Everything cool?"

"Nah. She dumped me."

"Aw. Ain't no thang. Hang tight. You at her pad or what?"

"I'll be at the old church across from the little store near her house."

"Church, huh? Damn, she really messed you up." Doug snickered before adding, "I'm on my way, alright?"

"Thanks, man." Adam hung up.

Adam had actually attended church with Michelle, her mother, and older sister Denise on Sunday mornings after having slept over on Saturday nights. Their church was on the far end of town: an even poorer neighborhood where rows of apartments surrounded the rundown brick building, with a large room for service and a small one used for Sunday school. On one side of the building, a quaint little cafeteria sold hot food and donuts, and after service, everyone crammed into it, with too few tables and a long line of people that weaved through the tables in a confused mess.

Usually, after they ate, the upholders of the faith would gather in the gravel parking lot. Young men stood together appraising each other's cars and bad-mouthing their children.

The women would huddle together and reminisce about the cousin who had gone off to college somewhere, or the one who went off to join the army. They would compliment each other's clothing, then go to join their boyfriends or husbands.

Before they'd leave, Adam would be introduced around. 'This is my boyfriend, Adam,' Michelle would say. Many of them responded with a mere smile, or with no reply at all, so Adam figured that after introductions, he'd be the subject of their conversations.

In person, Michelle displayed friendliness to everyone while secretly berating them all. 'I don't really talk to her because she gets on my nerves.' 'Did you see what *she* was wearing—you do not wear *that* to church.' '*That* girl can't keep a boyfriend.'

Listening to Michelle, her mom, and sister during the ride back was dreadful, and it didn't stop once they'd arrive home. Sometimes hours would pass, and Adam would watch television, tuning them out until he'd grow tired and then jump into his dirty little car and go home.

The church Adam stood by hadn't been used in years. Looking up at the cross on the roof's steeple, it appeared to drag slowly across the night sky. While narrow at the front, the building extended the length of the entire street to a blacktop parking lot in the back. The tan stone walls were darkened by cascades of run-off water that came down the sides of the entrance where a curved wooden door was recessed within an arch frame with ribbed moldings. On either side of the door, aged sheets of plywood covered the stained-glass windows, once pieced-together portraits of saints. The base of the building appeared sooty, while the crevasses between the stones were black with mold.

Adam placed a hand down on one of the soaked steps leading to the church entrance, and took a seat.

The gold foil, still attached to some of the plastic wrapping, floated into the darkness when Adam opened his cigarettes. He plucked one out by its spongy brown filter.

A police siren ululated somewhere nearby. Then came the soft murmur of a train in the distance. Adam was most distracted, though, by the persistent tinkling of a wind chime somewhere nearby.

Under the beams of streetlamps, a lustrous white Camaro grumbled as it came to a halt. Doug leaned over, opened the passenger door, and yelled, "Adam, get in the car!"

Adam stood and dusted off the seat of his pants.

The radio was on but turned down, and it emitted a bright blue fluorescence that expelled across the car's interior. Adam's backpack landed in the back seat and his pants made a rubbing sound against the leather as he fixed himself into the cradling passenger seat.

Doug glanced back before forming a U-turn, then accelerated down the stretch of road with the engine roaring at the thrust of each gear.

Resting his left wrist above the steering wheel, Doug leaned his right elbow on the armrest between the two seats, turned his shaved head toward Adam, and leisurely began stroking his overgrown beard.

"So, she dumped ya?"

Adam hung his head, staring at the black patch of seat material that formed a triangle between his legs. As he looked away, he lifted a hand to his face and tried not to think about her. With his finger resting on his lip, he breathed in the astringent aroma that comes with smoking. It was no different from the strong scent of smoke on his breath as he answered, "Yeah."

"Don't cry," Doug taunted.

Rain droplets had begun to collect on the windshield and Adam turned to look out the passenger window at the fragmented images as they swooshed by.

"Cheer up. Ya'll probably be back together before the weekend is over—you'll see. You know how it is."

Adam sat quietly.

"Don't go and get all salty," Doug added. "We're going to party, man. There'll be plenty of we'atches you can talk to."

Adam forced a smile.

Doug's hand thumped Adam's chest.

"I've got what you need," he said, then reached into the back seat.

Adam could hear the crimpling of a paper bag, followed by the clinking of bottles. The car drifted over and Doug straightened out with a quick jerk once he sat forward.

Doug held two large bottles with conical-shaped necks. He handed one to Adam, then opened his, resting it between his legs. The window rolled down and the bottle cap flew outside. Before the window had gone all the way back up, Doug tipped back his condensation-covered bottle when his phone rang in a song-tone. Doug gazed at the glowing screen before answering, "You best have my money, bitch!" He laughed.

Adam went to work on his bottle.

"Yeah, I'm on my way. I had to pick up Adam . . . We'll be there in a minute!"

Doug hung up, then took the onramp to the highway.

* * *

Everything appeared immaculate—the wide, smooth roads seemingly free of oil stains. The monstrous supermarket on the nearby shopping strip had ample parking and lights deemed suitable for a stadium. New restaurants with colorful lights and parking lots full of cars could be seen in either direction. Even the police drove sparkling new SUVs. One sat out of view behind a nondescript building, waiting for a weekend speeder.

Doug turned into a dark, placid road with large houses and yards looming with aged, sprawling oak trees. The Camaro approached Doug's house, where the lights outside accented the brick façade and complemented the overall elegant design. Doug coasted through the long driveway, and the motion-sensitive light on the side of the house came on as they passed through, exposing a beige recreational vehicle the size of a bus. The light stayed on until they reached a boat and trailer near the garage.

While there was plenty of space in Doug's house, he lived in the guesthouse constructed over the two-car garage.

They parked and got out.

Adam stood on the driveway, looking into the prim yard redolent with fresh vegetation. Doug's mother maintained a small garden of vegetables and flowers. Arrays of red and marigold flowers aligned the brick wall behind the house and continued down the length of the stained wooden fence. Stone steps led from the house to a pergola in the middle of the yard, and behind that stood a stone birdbath.

"You want your bag?" Doug asked. He was hunched over, emptying his back seat.

"Well, can I crash here tonight, if it's cool with your folks?"

"Sure," Doug said, still leaning into his car. He struggled to carry the bottles out, all while holding the backpack as it swung from one finger. He reached a hand out and handed Adam his backpack, then lifted a bent knee and closed the door

There was a long row of wooden steps on the side of the garage and when they reached the top, Doug unlocked the windowpane door. Inside, his computer monitor glowed while sitting on a high table with a padded stool. The table itself was inherently non-functional as it was covered in a multitude of drawings: some incomplete, some penciled, some inked. The edge of the table was a metropolis of markers, map pencils, and every size brush available. On the ground near the table stood clear containers deluged with packs of colored pencils, cases of markers, pastels, and an airbrush gun and hose.

Doug slipped out of his shoes, then chilled the beers in the refrigerator.

"Should I take off my shoes?" Adam asked.

"Only if it makes you feel better."

"I'll just wait here on the rug."

Adam stood in the living room where the walls had been completely covered with Doug's artwork. The picture closest to the entrance was a penciled drawing of two squirrels.

Adam was looking closely at it when Doug came over and explained that one morning he had been standing at the top of the stairs, smoking, when he looked across the alley to the neighbor's yard. Grabbing his drawing pad at the perfect moment, he had captured two squirrels in early morning copulation. The drawing had been in an exhibit once and, underneath, a white card read: Just a squirrel, trying to get a nut.

Doug chuckled, then he went to the bathroom, leaving the door open, and slapped on the lights.

"I'm just going to change my shirt," Doug called out.

Adam finished his drink and turned the empty bottle, rotating it slowly in his hands.

Doug came out buttoning his bright habanera shirt but stopped, looked at it and went back to his room.

Adam heard Doug's closet slide open and in an instant he emerged from the darkness of the bedroom.

Doug crossed the living room, this time in a black tee, then slipped into his everyday shoes. Instead of asking, he simply took Adam's bottle, along with the one he had left on his table, and disposed of them in the kitchen. He brought out two more bottles from the fridge.

Doug handed Adam both bottles, then stroked his thighs, drying his hands from the condensation. He retrieved his keys from nearby, then turned off the lights. They were ready.

Outside, Doug fussed as he struggled with the door to his car, the keys jingling between each profane verse, as he had somehow broken the keyless remote. They eventually got in and Doug started the engine.

Adam held the bottles as he watched Doug

meddle with his phone and make a call.

"I had to change my shirt . . . I was in my white shirt with the big hole in the back . . ." Doug said. "My old jeans . . ." Doug turned to make faces at Adam as he listened. "Just wait, I'll be right there. I'm outside the house." He reversed into the street and drove away.

After Doug hung up, he shoved the phone into his pocket and reached for his bottle.

Adam handed it over.

"Girlfriend always sweating my nuts. Don't you hate that?"

"No," Adam replied. "Mine is sweating someone else's"

"My bad. I didn't mean to—" Doug waited. "Never mind."

They drove through a neighborhood where the street was crammed with cars.

Doug fiddled with his phone. He put the device to his ear and spoke. "Hey. Where are we supposed to park?" As he drove, he scanned both sides of the street. "Oh, alright."

Big Bird and the Cookie Monster stood waving on the wall of the daycare Doug turned into, where he parked.

Adam and Doug stepped out and stood near the car as Gabrielle approached. Although she was too far to make out clearly, her petite figure and pallid skin distinguished her well. After she crossed the road, she peered down walking through the clumpy lawn leading to the daycare parking lot.

She was close enough now that Adam could see her ruddy hair had a part to one side, pulled back tightly and clipped together. A pierced navel peeked out under her violet backless top that fit snug around her waist and cupped her breasts. The top tied together at the base of her neck. As she crossed the parking lot, her toeless shoes tapped the floor.

Doug and Adam met her halfway.

"Shit, Doug, it took you long enough."

Doug pecked her on the mouth.

Gabrielle pulled away. "Hi, Adam," she said, giving him a quick wave that revealed brightly painted fingernails.

"Hey, Gabby."

They walked toward the house, one Adam didn't recognize, and Doug had taken Gabrielle's hand.

Once they were inside, Gabrielle shut the door.

Adam looked around at the furniture in the empty living room. He walked through the house and heard the crowd of people in the backyard.

Gabrielle and Doug chatted behind him as they walked.

"Did you get any weed?" she asked.

"Yeah, but it's schwag."

"Bobby has some Dro. Me, Kim, and Nichole smoked a blunt with him and his friend. I only hit it twice, and it got me stoned."

"You want me to get some? René has some real hydro. He'll hook it up."

"Nah. By the time you get back, the party would be over. Everybody has weed. We'll get by."

They arrived at the backyard, and Doug gave a conceding nod, showing Adam to head toward the open garage lit inside with a soft bulb.

Two girls argued as Adam passed them on the driveway, leading to the garage.

Wires fed into the backside of a large stereo blaring music with deep bass and rapid snares. The voice sounded muzzled and angry; Doug sang along as they crossed the open garage door. The music, however, was no match for the boisterous laughing from a group of women nearby.

Plastic coolers had been placed against a wall inside the garage.

Doug reached into the cooler and brought out

two dark bottles, then handed one to Adam.

Adam set down the bottle; he still hadn't finished the one he'd brought with him.

While they stood there, Doug leaned over toward Gabrielle.

All Adam could see was a moving jaw as Doug whispered a few things into his cupped hand.

Gabrielle gave an empathetic, "Aww," then went to hug Adam.

Adam stood impassive as she hooked her arms around his shoulders. She stepped back and looked him in the eyes.

"Don't worry about her. You're too good for her. I already told you that. We'll find you a pretty girl. A nice one. Right, Doug?"

Doug gave a wide-eyed look. "Oh, yeah! I know lots of girls."

Gabrielle turned her look into a scowl before she shot an angry glance at Doug.

"Let's go sit over there," Doug said, fisting a bottle, and pointing a finger toward an alluring blue swimming pool lit from within. He greeted everyone along the way and collected one or two persons from each social circle to join him at the glass patio table on the far end of the pool. Once seated, Doug made introductions.

Afterward, a tanned blonde, apparently named Tammy, arrived at the round table. She reached for the center of the table, and with her hands on the hors d'oeuvres, said, "Let me get these out of your way." She rolled her eyes. "My dad," she said as she departed.

Doug and a friend discussed cars.

The guys next to Adam spoke about something requiring hand pictorials. One motioned his hand in different directions, then they laughed.

A group of girls stood nearby, while two other girls sitting alongside the pool indulged in lively conversation.

Adam stared at one of them, studying her countenance as she listened to the one who was speaking.

"Adam!" Doug called.

Adam looked over at a bright orange ember at the base of a colorful smoking pipe held by Doug's friend, Jason.

Adam shunned it with a wave.

The pipe was passed over, where it was rekindled.

Adam asked if anyone wanted another drink, though no one seemed interested. He picked up a beer and strolled slowly through the backyard, hoping he'd see a familiar face.

Most of the gala was huddled around a folding table with a bottle of vodka in the center. Adam stood near the crowd and watched as someone suggested a drinking game.

"Name another word for dick," said Heather, a girl from school, "but you have five seconds or else you have to chug whatever you're drinking."

"Shlong," Heather started. She motioned a circle, indicating the order of the game.

"Weiner!"

"Love muscle!"

"My sex pistol!"

"Penis!"

"Um, uh. Uh . . ."

The crowd jeered. Some began counting down. The contestant didn't make it.

"Chug that shit!" someone called out.

Adam turned and noticed an empty chair outside the garage. He pulled the tab on a beer as he sat down, then watched two guys sitting nearby.

One removed his hands from his pockets, holding a clear baggie. He handed a bunched green ball to someone sitting beside him.

The stout guy set a piece of cardboard on his lap, then scrutinized the dry, wadded leaf before mincing it. "Go bring the pipe," he said, then he put some back into the bag as he waited.

Racing back, the skinny one held a long translucent purple cylinder. After tampering with the metallic cup, he positioned the pipe into his mouth. The shaft filled with condensed smoke as he sucked some of it in, holding it, then let it out in portions. After giving it another go, he passed the pipe to Adam, who had been staring.

Adam raised his beer in gesture only to realize he thought he needed another.

The thin one had been paying close attention, sitting beside his hefty friend. He took the lighter, and as he drew in smoke, his face became flush and the contraption slammed onto the cement floor as he let go. The sound of the crash could barely be heard over the cacophony of gasping and coughing. He darted off.

Still holding smoke, the heavy one let it out in one slow exhale as he started laughing, then got up to follow his buddy.

Jason walked by, gripping a cell phone to one ear.

"Hey, uh—" Jason snapped his fingers wildly. "Adam! Hey, you want to buy some shrooms? I'm picking up my friend and he's going to make a run—twenty dollars for an eighth." He peered down at Adam sitting in the chair. "Some of us are going halves," he added.

"Mmmm, no. I'm cool."

Only two steps away, Jason stopped, turned, and asked, "How about some X? They're twenty each."

Man, how can they afford this stuff? Adam thought.

"None for me. Thanks."

Doug went over and sat next to Adam. He stared at the pipe on the ground before he picked it up. "Somebody left this?" He furrowed his brow before lighting the remnants of the bowl. "Pretty good," he said, the words squeezed out as he held in smoke. "Try it, Adam."

"Nah."

Doug continued lighting the pipe.

Adam said, "My cousin smokes that crap. That's all he does."

Doug smiled. "Don't you know? Weed ain't addictive," he said, and lit up again.

"No. It's getting stoned that is."

Doug placed a hand on Adam's shoulder and chuckled while coughing. He grinned, shaking his head.

Without saying anything further, they got up.

Doug immersed himself into a nearby crowd.

Adam took another beer and loitered alone near

the garage as the party abated. It hadn't rained since Adam left Michelle's and the sky was completely clear now, but it felt humid and warm.

The table nearby had become covered by an accumulation of cans. When Adam sat at the table, he heard someone behind him say, "Hey Adam, come with me to the store."

He turned his head, saw who it was, and said, "No. I'm sorry, Kate, I can probably barely get up."

"O-kay, he just called me Kate," said Heather.

Heather asked another girl, standing near the table, and the two of them left.

Adam found himself sitting alone, and the backyard was empty except for the diehard patrons.

He got up and faltered over to Doug, who sat at the patio table. He asked if they could leave, but Doug suggested another beer.

"Not unless you want me throwing up in your car."

"You feel like you have to throw up?"

"*If* I have another beer."

"Alright, I'll let your stomach settle down before we leave. Just sit back, and if you have to go, go!"

Soon after, Doug had gotten up and Adam sat alone at the patio table with his head down over his folded arms. The alcohol flowed in his system. Adam's thoughts reverted to the night's earlier occurrences like old re-runs that were difficult to ignore. Adam felt *different*—aside from being drunk. He'd become single, against his will, and he felt robbed. Adam wanted to be at home in his room crying until his pillow became smeared with tears and runny mucus. He'd cry until he'd fall asleep with his eyes sore and drained.

Doug and Gabrielle came by.

"Adam!" Doug called.

Adam looked up. He stood and followed them back through the house to the front door.

Doug walked Gabrielle to her car on the far end of the street.

Adam waited on the concrete steps where the porch light above was being pelted by a persistent moth. The act of standing seemed difficult; Adam now felt the full effects of excess drinking. An arm covered his stomach, upset with gurgling fluids at the brink of eruption.

Doug returned and they left.

The stairs leading up to Doug's place seemed longer than usual. Adam took them slowly, one step at a time with a sickening effect that made him wish he could magically arrive at the top without effort. Once inside, he groped for the wicker chair and eased into the seat cushion.

Doug brought two folded blankets and a colorfully variegated glass pipe. He set the blankets on Adam's lap, passed him the pipe, and searched for his lighter.

Short on excuses, Adam took the pipe.

"We call this fag weed," Doug explained as he handed Adam the lighter.

Adam objected, pushing the pipe and lighter back to Doug.

"Come on, try it."

Adam gave in, and after inhaling, he let out a puff of smoke. "It tastes . . ."Adam said, as he smacked his mouth. "Fruity."

"Yeah, fag weed."

Immediately, Adam felt his eyelids swell. He didn't feel high—or maybe he couldn't tell. Nothing mattered anymore; he just wanted to sleep.

Doug pointed a derogatory finger at Adam. "HA! You're stoned," he said, then laughed.

Adam unfurled the blankets on the living room floor.

"Doug, thanks for letting me—" A yawn quelled

the rest of his statement.

"Stay? Any time."

Adam stretched himself out on the floor and fell asleep without even reaching for his blanket.

SEVEN

The row of living room windows glowed behind closed blinds, bright enough to wake Adam who lay on the floor with a blanket wrapped tightly around him. He felt the qualm of a hangover and wanted to sleep the rest of the day.

Doug went into the kitchen. He was shirtless, wearing his long cut-off shorts, and didn't bother to look over as he filled a glass from the faucet.

Adam sat up and moaned.

"Hey, Sunshine! I was wondering when you were getting up. How do you feel?" Doug said before taking a long pull of water.

"Okay," Adam croaked. "What time is it?"

"About . . ." Doug peeked over at the microwave. "Noon."

Adam got up, leaving behind the mess of blankets, and followed Doug through an open door to a room used as a painting studio. Doug's family was of Irish descent, and the walls of his studio were amassed with paintings of his heritage, including one of a castle in Ireland he claimed belonged to his family. The occult and Celtic symbols were among his favorite images to produce.

They walked around an easel centered directly under the room light. What looked like a child's wooden desk sat against the wall and on its surface was a tin case with different sized pencils, several drawings, and a smoldering cigarette on an ashtray. Doug sat in the office chair that had been lowered to match the desk, reached over, and held out a wide sheet so Adam could take it. "Check this out." He picked the cigarette up and the ember turned a bright orange, then smoke rose slowly from his mouth as he spoke. "I drew it yesterday."

Adam examined the upright boulders formed in a semi-circle like Stonehenge penciled life-like with different shades of darkness, contrasting the white background.

"I like the surface of the stone. It looks rough," Adam said, looking over the speckles and cracks on the stones in the drawing he held.

Doug stood, and pointed out the imperfections of the drawing Adam held, in the intrinsic way an artist finds flaws within their work. Then they stared at it admiringly, without saying a word. Human nature would also allow Doug the sensibility to marvel at his own creation, even if it wasn't perfect.

"Hey, Adam, did you notice something new in the living room?"

"No."

"Go see." Doug grinned as he went to the small desk and snapped the pencil box shut.

The painting was hard to miss, as large as it was, sitting in the living room where it leaned against a wall. Her laced corset stopped above a g-string where her curved napes showed the smallest variation of a crease atop her right thigh. She appeared to be adjusting one of her lace stockings with a dark line that formed a seam running up the back of each leg. She wore spike high-heels with one leg propped onto a wooden step.

Doug stood beside Adam, staring at the painting and currying his beard.

"What do you think? Does it make you horny?" Doug asked.

"Huh?"

"My friend wants her airbrushed on the hood of his truck."

Adam waited, trying not to sound zealous about the painted woman who had actually provoked lustful thoughts in his mind almost instantly upon seeing her, but he quickly cleared them out. "Her skin, it looks smooth. And her stockings—how'd you make them look so real?"

"That's the cool thing about paint. You can do effects that look real if you have the right brushes."

From outside, Doug's mother called in her distinct brogue voice.

"DOUGLOUS."

Doug sighed, and gave Adam a sideways glance. "My mother wants me to move this dresser thing—I don't know?"

Scanning the floor, Doug found his beat-up old shoes with the perpetually tied knots, and slipped into them. On his way to the door, he yanked a black t-shirt from off the messy table and held it by the shirttail, giving it two good flaps when she called again.

"DOOUGLOUUUS."

"You need some help?" Adam offered.

Doug opened the door, with the shirt in one hand

swinging pliantly as he moved. "Nah, it's my sister's. It's not that big. But thanks." He slapped at his bare stomach, the way a person would do when they're too full, then headed outside.

Adam peeked through the window blinds he'd pulled apart, just enough to see, without being seen.

Doug's mother stood on the back patio wearing a long-sleeved denim shirt that shrouded a pair of worn slacks. She stood with her arms crossed, watching Doug's six-year-old sister who ran across the patio in her pink ballerina dress. Short, auburn hair swirled to form a parasol of hair as Doug's sister began pirouetting barefoot on the lush yard.

Doug had reached the bottom of the steps when his shaved head burst through his t-shirt, with his arms inside struggling to find the sleeves. As he crossed the lawn, he rotated his shoulders, tugged and twisted his shirt, then walked into the house.

Doug's mother said something to Doug as he passed through the open sliding doors. She walked in after him and his sister skipped closely behind.

Adam moved away from the window and fished out the disheveled pack of cigarettes from his pants pocket. The cigarette he pulled out had a bent tip, and Adam lit it awkwardly from one side of his mouth. On the first drag his mouth filled with the astringent taste of bitter smoke, causing him to gag. Adam rushed into the bathroom where he began spitting into the toilet, waiting to throw up. Nothing came out, and Adam leaned against the tile wall waiting for the feeling to pass, careful not to inhale the smoke from the lit cigarette in his hand. He dropped the cigarette into the toilet and watched it spin before disappearing at the bottom of the bowl.

Adam crumpled and tossed the wadded pack into the empty wastebasket beside the commode. It appeared too obvious there, so he picked it out of the trash can and took it to the garbage compactor in the kitchen instead.

He left the kitchen and made his way toward the wicker chair in front of the TV. Adam grabbed the remote, plopped onto the round cushion, and pressed the power button. Nothing happened. Adam realized the remote was to the satellite dish, so he turned the TV on the old-fashioned way, then sat back down and surfed the channels.

Adam was on the third or fourth round of channels when Doug walked in, sucking at his teeth with loud smacks.

Doug rubbed his stomach. "My mom says go

down and eat," he said as he passed Adam.

"No thanks."

"She made pancakes and bacon. I ate a stack this big." Two flat hands displayed the imaginary stack, then he turned away. In his studio, Doug snapped shut a container, moved a few things, and turned off the lights. He walked out and closed the door.

As he passed through the kitchen, Doug dropped his cup into the sink where a splash of water could be heard going down the pipe. He then stopped at the messy table and placed pencils and other art utensils in precise order, dropping brushes into their containers and popping container lids open and shut. He pulled the wooden stool from underneath the messy table and it creaked as he mounted it.

"I told my mom about you and Michelle," Doug said.

Adam turned halfway around in his chair. "What'd she say?"

Doug shuffled papers and put a stack of drawings to one side. "That 'you can't force someone to love you and you shouldn't try'."

Adam turned his attention back toward the TV, unaware he was speaking out loud. "Hm, interesting proverb."

Doug looked up from a painting he held. "What?"

"A proverb," Adam reiterated.

"Is that like a cliché?"

"No. Well, kind of. A proverb is a saying that states something obvious or true."

Adam ignored the cats in the commercial on television, choosing his words carefully.

"A cliché is more like an overused phrase, or something unnecessary. You know what I mean? Like, 'you know what I mean'."

"Uh-huh."

Doug slid off the stool. He reached into his pocket for his phone, dialed a number and as he waited, he tugged on the belt loop of his shorts.

"Hey, rat face," he said loud enough that it made a reverberating sound on the walls, then he disappeared into the bedroom.

Adam made himself comfortable as a promising case on a detective show had begun.

"BULLSHIT," Doug said from his room, followed by laughter.

Still on the phone, he came out to the fridge and guzzled orange juice straight from the carton.

By the time the first case had finished, Doug was back at the messy table, while still on the phone.

"So we're just going hang out? Alright, cool. Just call me back . . . No, I'll be out by then . . . Okay, love you, too."

Doug set the phone down, then went to shower. He was out ten minutes later wearing an oversized towel like a sarong as he passed through the living room.

"Whenever you feel like showering, the bathroom's right there," Doug motioned, throwing his head back toward the open door.

Adam watched him pinch water away from the bridge of his nose, then he turned to face the television again. "Oh, hey, Doug!" Adam turned back.

"Yeah?"

"I don't mean to bug you . . ."

"What is it?"

"You wouldn't happen to have a spare toothbrush I could have?"

"Under the sink, where I keep my supplies," Doug said. "Help yourself."

"I appreciate it."

"Don't act like you don't know, Adam, *mi casa*—"

Doug was dressing in his room when the phone rang again.

Adam was engrossed with forensics—blood

stains, traces of hair, missing persons, and complaints from neighbors about the smell of decaying bodies—when Doug came over.

Doug stood behind Adam's chair, tucking his green polo shirt into a pair of new blue jeans. The belt around his waist jingled as it waved back and forth.

"Adam!"

Adam looked over.

"You want to do something tonight? I'm going to Gabrielle's but her mom's being a bitch. She won't let her go out so looks like it'll just be you and me."

"Okay."

Doug tugged at his shirttail little by little until it came out entirely. He let out a sigh, and headed for the door where he slid into his old shoes.

"I'll be back around nine—make it ten, alright?" Doug said, on his way out.

After hearing the complete scale of thudding stairs, Adam got up, wedged the blinds apart, and watched Doug get into his car.

Adam was watching the Three Stooges engaged in a serenade, *'sweetie, honey, baby doll . . . QUIET, YOU!'* when Doug's house phone rang.

"Hello?"

"What are you doing?" It was Doug.

"Watching TV."

"You ready?"

"Yeah."

"Did you take a shower?"

"Yeah, but I'm wearing the same clothes."

"Hey, guess what?"

"What?"

"Gabrielle's mom took off with her boyfriend to some log cabin in Hill Country. She won't be back until Monday."

"Oh, okay."

"I'm going crash here so I won't be able to take you home until tomorrow. Is that cool?"

"Sure. No problem."

"Alright. If anyone calls, tell them to call me on my cell."

"Alright."

"So what are you going do, just watch TV all night?"

"Probably."

"There's some forties in the fridge."

"I'm fine. I just feel like chilling."

Doug smirked. "Okay. We're about to make a run, so I'll see you tomorrow."

Adam asked shyly, "Hey, Doug?"

"Yeah?"

"How can I order a pizza?"

"Yeah, the number is on speed dial, 7—no, 6. You'll have to go and wait for it, or it'll come to my mom's house."

"Thanks, I'll do that."

"Later."

Adam hung up, and he sat smiling at the revelation of having Doug's place all to himself. A part of him felt guilty for wanting to be alone in someone else's house, but a sense of excitement immediately quelled any bad feelings he'd had.

Moving freely throughout the house, Adam took a shower, brushed his teeth with one of the new toothbrushes he'd found under the sink, then *really* put on the same clothes, only he decided to change his shirt. He reached into his backpack and brought out the anime shirt he'd bought the day before, still new, with the tags.

As soon as he was dressed, Adam grabbed the phone and ordered a large, thin-crust, hamburger and jalapeño pizza with a two-liter Coke and waited by the window for the car to arrive.

The driveway was longer than Adam had expected, and if he hadn't jogged the last half, the pizza man would have made it to the door of the main house.

"Hey!" Adam called.

The pizza man looked at the front door, then back at Adam, who held a folded twenty out to him. The man met Adam halfway across the lawn. "Alright, that's $13.52," he said, then took the bill.

Adam gave him two bucks tip and walked back mesmerized by the greasy box in his hands.

He ate while standing in the kitchen and didn't bother to look away from the pizza as he ripped through it like someone in an eating contest. Only after the pizza had ceased to exist did Adam stop to fill his cup with ice and drowned the crushed pieces in sudsy cola.

Full and content, Adam sat through an old Dirty Harry movie where he'd been hunted down by cyborg cops on motorcycles, but Harry seemed to cleverly outwit them all using only his .44-caliber Magnum. With a woman accomplice at his side, he was in some ways similar to James Bond—without the fancy gadgets, of course.

'This must be your lucky day, punk.' While Clint didn't say that in this movie, Adam certainly felt lucky. He was proud of himself for not having thought about Michelle until now. Even now, as he looked back, he didn't seem to miss her. It didn't seem as bad as it had the day before, and Adam reminded himself of another cliché, 'it could always be worse'. Hanging out at Doug's place, eating pizza, and watching satellite television was better than being at home—especially now, when he'd be sulking over Michelle.

Adam stayed up until the airwaves were under the dominance of the especially cheesy brand of melodramatic commercials, like the one of the bloated red-faced man urging everyone to run down to his furniture warehouse for the one-day-only sale that ran each week, or the phone company that promised to give anyone a line even if they failed to pay for prior service, or the lawyers with paid actors telling their accounts of big paydays, and the one of the ninety-year-old woman who could scale Mt. Everest on her motorized cart, then holler the name of the scooter company from atop the great mountain.

Adam yawned. He turned off the television, used the bathroom, arranged his blankets, and finally lay down.

The house was dark and quiet, and it wasn't long before he was asleep.

White light is diffused over a field of green knolls with

dabs of white and yellow flowers that bend under the will of a salty breeze. Strung across the hilly plane is a parapet of slate stones. A hazy white figure appears on the stone wall, far away. The apparition comes closer, then with sheer clarity, it becomes evident the figure is a woman. She's dressed in full trousseau, walking the wall barrier. Blonde curls escape the back of her neatly styled French roll, made elegant with a coruscating tiara. The shimmering satin crepe fits closely to her haunch and outlines the contours of her body. Flowing behind her, a veil train flaps and uncoils like a lofty flag. She's smiling, holding a bouquet in one hand and waving slowly with the other. She turns around and steps off.

Adam pounces toward the rocky wall. His chest skids, and his splayed hands graze the surface. Pebbles from the stone wall follow her as she falls hundreds of feet to the craggy ebb below. As she plummets, her bouquet trails her body, appearing like a lowercase i against the dark water and crashing waves. Adam turns with a flinch to elude watching her fate.

Adam opens his eyes only to see the pale purple walls of a run-down corridor. Where's the bride? Looking back, the stone wall she leapt off is now just a mere fraction of the size, however, the image is still sharp and lively though it sits in a tarnished gold frame done in intricate tracery and hangs on a purple wall. A white light begins emanating from the picture until it engulfs the frame. Slowly devouring the wall, the light seeps to the very edges of the painting before deepening like a perpetual flux. The hole becomes as big as the wall. Adam steps forward, and the white retreats like a scared creature.

The floor gives way to a mass of darkness, then suddenly Adam is surrounded by an immensity of slender stalks in a decaying forest. Unnaturally cold, the air strokes his motionless skin. A child squalls in the distance, it sounds like Mommy *though the cries are incomprehensible. The crying stops only to be replaced by a croaking frog. A step backwards arouses something flesh-like, possibly a limb. It springs upward in a powerful thrust and before Adam can move, he's caught. His eyes widen as he sees the slithering body of a glowing eel wrapped around Adam's arms. It pins his wrists together before dragging him, arms first, into the earth. Sand smothers Adam's face, stinging his eyes and clogging his nasal openings as he tries frantically to breathe. His hands are pinned, burrowed in the ground. A vague light breaks through the surface and the ground gives way.*

Adam now finds himself in a desert of massive sand dunes. Trying to climb up one of the dunes takes several attempts as the sand melts away while clambering its side. Once at the top, Adam can see the desolate street of a penury town. He climbs down, then walks over rickety baseboards that form the floor between two cement buildings.

It could be Mexico, maybe the Philippines, or Lebanon—they all look the same. Adam walks through a passage where two shops are coalesced. The door is made of a metal frame with welded sheets of metal once painted blue. The door opens and Adam proceeds through.

A woman sits in a wooden rocking chair, pushing herself gently. She stops to look at Adam and crosses her badly varicose-veined legs. Around the woman are ornaments of stuffed papier-mâché frogs in trios with little instruments and sombreros; some are holding beer bottles. Ceramic statuettes and painted piggy banks also collectively surround the room. The woman stairs lazily through her square framed glasses, as she fans herself. She's pregnant, and Adam knows she's never giving birth to the fetus, fully developed, now black and hardened like an eight-pound piece of coal. The woman doesn't speak, not verbally, although she transmits words through telepathy. She says there's a young man Adam must save. His name is unsaid but he will be unmistakably recognized. He's a young student who is soon to be bludgeoned to death by the locals after they proclaim him guilty of fornication. Adam starts to explain that he's had this dream before and he knows what the outcome will be.

A filthy-looking boy serving as harbinger bursts through the door. He says a group of soldiers are approaching, and scampers off. The woman steadies her hands to her temples and melts away into a white haze.

Adam stands in the foyer of a university and his clothing smells of burnt electrical wire. There he is, the guy, speaking to his soon-to-be revolting mob. Adam explains the situation to the student but he refuses to go. The student's dismay came only after the crowd turns unruly. Adam takes him through the back where they escape unharmed and they arrive at a dusty-looking red sports car. The guy extends an arm to shake Adam's hand, but Adam urges him to leave immediately and never come back.

No sooner is the red sports car out of sight, does a white truck with four soldiers park behind Adam. They climb down and close the doors, drawing weapons as they corner Adam. There is nowhere to go. The soldier on one side pumps his shotgun and the other keeps his hand over his revolver close to his thigh. The soldier facing Adam has a machete and asks where the student went. Adam doesn't answer. The machete brakes air with a low swoosh, and Adam feels the bone cracking THUAP as he moans, trying not to cry out loud.

Dangling painfully by a swath of flesh, the machete removed his left arm and Adam holds it firmly. The deep gash soaks his hand red and the air becomes sour with the smell of warm blood. Adam drops to his knees in hope he's shot, though it's too late. He realizes the man with the blood-dripping machete comes over to Adam's side. The soldier steps back, then swings for Adam's neck, only it misses, breaking his jaw as the blade sinks into the side of Adam's face.

A woman shrieks in the background.

The incubus vanished.

Adam sat up and took in deep breaths of cool air, feeling his heart racing and his chest expand with each breath. The room was dark with the exception of the soft lights coming off Doug's computer sitting on the messy table.

Adam lay on the floor and waited for his breathing to ease. Several minutes passed before he closed his eyes again; this time, he sojourned to the nether-land of dreamless sleep.

Birds crooned and warbled as they splashed and wallowed playfully in the birdbath below. Sunlight shown through the scantly opened blinds to form a corrugated pattern on Doug's artwork, mounted on the wall. According to the time on the DVR in the living room, it was 8:51 a.m.

Adam got up and went to the bathroom to relieve himself. He came back to the living room and sat on the wicker chair, then contemplated his next move. While he could wait for Doug to take him home, Adam decided it was time to leave.

The sheets were folded, and placed into Doug's closet.

Adam put away the remains from last night dinner. A cup went into the sink, and the empty pizza box went into the trash. Adam decided to take a shower after seeing his muddled hair, flattened on the sides and sticking out in the back.

After a long shower, he changed into a white undershirt, though the pants would endure yet another day. He folded his new shirt, being that its wear-span had been just a few hours; he could put it on again later without having to wash it first.

Warm air made its inversion into the cool room as Adam opened the door to leave. With his backpack on, he stepped outside and closed the door.

EIGHT

Doug's neighborhood was pleasantly quiet. The brick homes were ornately decorated with trimmed bushes, elaborate flowerbeds, and tall oak trees shading the green lawns. Adam passed the admirable houses with a sense of guilt, knowing he was somewhere he didn't belong.

At the end of the quiet street, he turned and headed toward the main road. He wasn't sure how to get to the light rail station that would take him home, but he knew this road would lead him there somehow. Adam found his bearings using the recognizable landscape. *The bank is on* that *side, so I need to head* that *way, then I make a left at the light,* Adam thought.

There were few cars in the parking lots of the

shopping centers, and the main road remained vacant with the exceptional boisterous car that sped past Adam, who ambled by on the sidewalk.

Adam observed the nondescript scenery of retail stores and it wasn't long before he reached the streetlight. There, he crossed the street, made a left, and continued for almost an hour before he saw the arched awnings that ascended over the train station and served as a sign he'd gone the right way.

The station looked fairly new, with blanched concrete floors and brightly-colored clusters of mosaic tile that decorated the round columns spanning across the boarding platform and supporting the metal awnings above. Two teenage girls in shorts and t-shirts stood near the ticket machine, waiting for the train. Adam walked over and bought a ticket that he could use for the train ride downtown and again at the transfer station leading home.

The train rolled in, then came to a stop, and with a hiss, opened a multitude of doors. Adam got on and sat by a window, as most seats were empty.

The train accelerated, and soon Adam could see the backs of buildings along the tracks as the plain walls with electric meters sped by. As they passed the back of a restaurant, it reminded Adam he was hungry, but he'd eat something once he got home.

"Home," he uttered the word to himself, staring out the window watching the houses that passed, wondering what the families inside were like. Adam pictured a father nudging his son to get out of bed lest he miss breakfast, like the one Doug's mother had made, and a little sister with a radiant smile; perhaps she told jokes in the mornings and made everyone laugh.

Adam rode along patiently, absentmindedly listening to the whirring wheels and clacking sounds coming from below, until the train made a stop.

A man wearing a dark shirt and black jeans that had been washed to a charcoal color walked through the sliding doors. He spoke loudly on his phone and bent forward as he laughed before sitting in one of the backwards facing seats. The loud man kicked his feet up but kept his heard turned back. Adam felt the man watching him from behind a set of dark shades.

The train sped off again and soon it crossed a high bridge leading into a labyrinth of tall and low-lying buildings.

Once downtown, Adam leaned over to look up at the prominent buildings in their illusory way they seemed to taper off at the top where they disappeared into the sky. The train passed through a tunnel, then came to an intersection where it stopped at a red light. Adam noticed a sign on the window of a store that caught his attention. At the next station, he got off.

The man on the phone stood, and followed.

Adam walked to the end of the station and stopped, waiting for the opposite train to pass while the man continued straight, now yelling into his phone.

Adam crossed the tracks.

The shop was located at the base of an old building, with a glossy finish on the walls sustained by several coats of dark paint. The brush marks left sloppy streaks around the small windows where the signs were displayed. The large sign that had gotten Adam's attention said, CHECKS CASHED. The smaller sign was of a chips-and-soda deal, where the price had been handwritten on a predisposed circle.

The concrete steps leading to the store had metal plates embedded onto them to prevent slipping, in an antiquated way that was perhaps more dangerous than it was functional. Adam took the steps and walked through the heavy wooden door with burglar bars on its interior.

Inside, the shop was crammed with snack stands, leaving almost no room to walk through. Near the entrance, different kinds of candy surrounded the tightly enclosed register. The fridge against the wall formed a variegated array of cans and bottles, and in front of the fridge was an aisle with mismatched items like Ramen noodles, bath soap, and car oil. Adam stood behind a man wearing baggy jeans and a dingy tank-top.

"Man, you not gone let me take this beer, for five cents?" the man argued with the cashier.

"You need a neeko," the cashier, an Asian man, insisted.

"I ain't got it! Look, count it. Two thirty-one." The customer said the numbers slowly, pushing the change across the counter.

"You need fi' cent."

"Man, ain't you got one of dem penny-deals, people leave pennies on?" He motioned with a finger, then looked around the counter.

"No!" The Asian man scowled. "That is for pennies—not neekos."

"Come on, man, I'll get you next time."

The cashier watched the man with a piercing stare.

"Cool?" the customer said, waiting.

"You go! You no come back here."

After the customer left with the beer in hand, the Asian man said some things in his native tongue Adam couldn't understand, but he understood enough to know they weren't pleasant.

"Can I help you?" he asked Adam, a tinge of anger still left in his tone.

"I just want to cash my check." Adam reached into his back pocket and pulled out a folded paycheck.

The cashier took the check, unfolded it, and looked at it closely, turning it to one side, and said, "I charge three percent."

Adam shrugged. "Okay."

The Asian man turned around and opened the door to a small room the size of a closet. The box-like structure was enclosed with raw wood and unpainted wood siding, where notices and sheets of papers had been taped to its sides. The man worked inside, near a one-way window facing the register.

While Adam waited, he glanced over at the lottery tickets in their dispensers located behind the register, over various magazines covered in black plastic, on a lower rack.

The man came back, and minus the three percent fee, Adam got $234.22. He thanked the man and left.

Leg-traffic on the sidewalk was unusually busy. Adam dodged a few people and walked around one of the small trees with a square grate on the floor surrounding the small trunk. He didn't come downtown much since there was hardly anything to do. With the exception of a few small fast food restaurants, there were mostly businesses located there. Adam passed a sandwich shop with neon lights in the windows and promotional banners over the entrance, followed by a half-empty parking lot before arriving at the corner. Cars and trucks passed as he waited. They stopped, and he made his way across the large street.

Adam turned and walked along a wall where a large shadow cast down over the sidewalk directly behind a brick building. On the floor were several homeless persons. Some lay on the street on dirty sleeping bags or layered blankets, huddled closely to garbage bags containing their worldly possessions. Farther on, a few squalid men stood together at the end of the sidewalk. Over to one side was a homeless couple, a tall man with a beard pulling a cart, and a woman with matted blonde hair.

A bicycle whizzed down the sidewalk and Adam moved over, having to step over a set of legs covered in a plaid blanket as dark and dirty as the ground beneath. The various men at the end of the sidewalk watched Adam as he walked by and he hoped they wouldn't accost him for change. *Just a few more steps and I'll be clear of them,* he thought.

At the next corner, he waited for more traffic until the light changed. Adam crossed the street and passed a McDonald's swarmed with gray pigeons, cooing.

Past the McDonald's was a small park with benches and a row of box-shaped pots that housed finely primmed bushes.

A man leaned against one of the pots with his butt perched on the edge, and his hands resting to either side of him. He looked around slowly, checking both ends of the sidewalk. His black hair was completely disheveled, and his arms were dark appearing as if used motor oil had dried over them. Suddenly, the man fixed his attention on something. He bolted across the street, not looking for traffic before he ran. The sound of his lumbering footsteps resonated loudly as he slowed moments before crashing into a glass wall. He chased his reflection on the glass building, stopping at the end of the sidewalk where he began yelling at himself, threatening to punch the glass. The man turned away, walked slowly in the direction he came from, then ran back, irately yelling at his image in the glass again.

Adam kept the man in his peripheral vision until he made it to the end of the street. Across the street, on the next corner, was the Greyhound bus station. A door facing the corner of the sidewalk was propped open.

Adam crossed the street. He'd meant to walk to the transfer station a few streets down, but slowed and walked into the bus station lobby instead.

The lobby had several florescent lights that were out. Adam walked along the wall lined with glass panes that looked into the street, then he passed a television that was mounted close to the ceiling showing a sitcom with no sound. He stood in line behind a woman in leggings waiting with a teenage girl dressed in her pajamas. Each had a piece of wheeled luggage to one side.

The ticket seller was helping a woman with a tan baseball cap and earrings the size of magician's rings.

Adam looked at the bus schedule displayed

behind the ticket counter. He started with the A's and saw that a bus to Abilene left in an hour and arrived four hours later. Adam had never been there, but he thought he could go there and come back by night time and no one would even know he'd taken a bus trip to another town. The thought amused him.

Adam finally approached the ticket seller, and stared at her gold tooth and bright eye shadow, before finally saying, "I'll take a ticket for the next bus to Abilene."

She looked at him wearily, then typed at her computer. "It's going be $54.25, Sugar," she said before patting the short, golden curls on the back of her head.

Adam paid, then went to sit down, passing the people who were now standing in line. He walked down a row of hard plastic chairs suspended over a long bar and sat across from an elderly Hispanic woman. She wore a shapeless blue dress and slept with her fingers interlocked over a paunch stomach. Her head was swathed in a veil, tilted back, with her mouth gaped.

The ticket was in a white envelope, and Adam unzipped his backpack he'd set between his legs and put the envelope inside, then leaned back in his chair and read over a few signs meant to prevent teenagers from running away.

The old woman's head rolled over and Adam heard her snoring.

A fly buzzed nearby and he shooed it away. The plump, red-eyed fly landed on the woman's pudgy face. Adam watched the black speck travel down the side of her face avoiding its deathtrap until it went inside through the side of her mouth. The woman swallowed it with a few masticating smacks, then continued sleeping.

The bus arrived, and parked along the side of the building.

Adam walked down the sidewalk and headed for the front of the bus as it boarded passengers. The exhaust was warm and odorous as it wafted from the rear of the bus. Adam waited for the few passengers to board. He handed over his ticket, went up the steps, and took a seat near the front.

Seated and ready, the bus drove out of the lot, squeezing through tight corners before taking one of the downtown streets and finally merging onto the highway. It merged slowly, letting cars pass before picking up speed. Adam sat comfortably and looked out the window at the scope of buildings as they drove.

It was almost an hour before the bus stopped at a plain-looking building that served as a station, with just a few cars outside. They picked up a few more passengers who boarded slowly. First was a young couple followed by an elderly man, and a young mom cradling a baby came onboard after him. The door closed and the final passenger, a teenage girl, looked each way at the empty seats, deciding to sit next to Adam.

"Hi," she said, smiling at him.

Adam looked over and smiled. Even while sitting down he could tell she was a lot shorter than he was. She had short hair, and was clad in a pink sleeveless shirt and tiny jean shorts.

The bus left again, and the two sat quietly.

Adam adjusted one of the curtains on his window to keep light from shining directly onto his face.

"Where you from?" she finally asked.

Adam responded, then asked where she was going and discovered they were both headed for Abilene.

"Do you ever come to Funky Town?" she asked, referring to Fort Worth, a neighboring city west of Dallas.

"No," Adam said, wanting to be left alone.

"I come here almost every week," she said. "I live with my aunt in Abilene, but my mom lives here so I visit her on the weekends."

She was in her early teens, but had the cognizance of a person who grew up too fast. Adam recognized it in himself.

After Adam remained silent for a while she didn't say anything else about her aunt or mother. She placed her hands on her bare legs and looked around.

"I've got a joke book." She reached into a small bag she'd placed by her feet. "It's dirty jokes, but they're kind of funny," she said, eagerly.

She turned to the first few pages, smiled, then asked, "Why does a bride smile on her wedding day?"

"I don't know," Adam said, amusing her.

"Because she doesn't have to give blow jobs anymore."

Adam smiled, but tried not to laugh for fear someone had heard her.

She paused for a moment, reading another line from her book. "What did the left nut say to the right nut? Don't talk to the guy in the middle. He's a prick." She laughed.

Adam watched her, smiling.

"What kind of meat does a priest have on Fridays? Nun." She giggled and turned a page. "That wasn't that funny. What's long, hard, and . . ." After a few more attempts, she stopped.

Adam hadn't laughed much, so she put the book away.

The bus became quiet.

Adam looked out the window as the bus slowed and he could see road construction ahead.

Adam thought about home, and in particular, an incident when he'd pushed his mother away from his little sister, Victoria, who'd been whimpering while pinned against a wall. With one arm, Adam—who was much stronger—pushed his mother back and she didn't resist much.

"Why are you fighting?" he'd said, looking at his mother.

Victoria managed to slip away, retreating to her room, slamming the door shut behind her.

Holding a long ash in one hand, Adam's mother had walked over to the sink and flicked it carelessly over a heap of dirty dishes. Adam could see her chest heaving slowly as she breathed. A cold stare was fixed on Adam's chest, only because it stood between her and Victoria's door. She took one last drag before looking Adam in the eyes—he wasn't moving. The television had been left on, and she returned to the living room.

Adam knocked on Victoria's door.

A distressed voice said, "It's open."

She had been packing drawers full of clothing into a gym bag.

"What's going on?" he asked as he walked in, closing the door behind him. "Why are you guys fighting?"

"It's her. I can't stand it here. I'm leaving."

"Come on, Vicky, don't do anything stupid. It'll all be okay," he assured her.

"She never even tells me she loves me or anything. She doesn't even care." She began to cry, huddled in a ball against the dresser.

Adam knelt beside Victoria and hugged her. He patted her back gently as she sobbed on his shoulder and dampened his shirt with tears.

"Look," Adam said. He pulled away and reached inside his pocket, then handed Victoria a few bills, around twenty dollars. "Why don't you spend the night at Julia's house, rent some movies, go get a hamburger or a pizza or whatever you want. Everything will be better tomorrow, okay?"

She looked at the money, then at Adam to ascertain his intentions were, in fact, sincere.

Victoria took the money and her friend's car picked her up shortly after.

Adam felt sorry for his little sister because he knew girls were emotionally sensitive, and they desired their mother's love all the time; it was different with boys.

The girl had fallen asleep with her head on Adam's shoulder while curled up against him.

The bus had started moving again but slowed as it got off the highway. There weren't many buildings around, and the fields they passed were arid and yellow, made up of wilted dry grass. On the service road, the bus continued to slow when Adam felt it stutter awkwardly.

The passengers began questioning each other; it was obvious now that the bus was coming to a definite stop.

Adam looked out his window, wondering what had happened when the sound of a speaker crackled.

The driver announced, "We seem to have broke down, ladies and gentlemen. I'll open the door if you'd like to stretch your legs. There's another bus on its way and it'll take you the rest of the trip. We're not far from our stop, but it might be another hour before the next bus arrives. Sorry for the delay."

The passengers reacted with moans and words of discontent.

Adam couldn't remember the girl's name sitting beside him.

She glanced back toward the end of the bus, then looked at Adam.

"I'm going to go walk around outside," he told her.

"Okay," she said, then moved her legs over, allowing Adam to get by.

Outside, Adam watched as a man smoked and a pair of children chased each other around on the dirt lot that had been dug up while under construction. Piles of dirt had been pushed to the sides, clearing a square section outlined by rebar poles and a black plastic that formed a retaining barrier that came all the way to the side of the road where the bus sat with its blinkers flashing.

Adam crossed over deep ruts in the ground, in search of a flat area where he could wait, but as he moved farther and farther, he found himself walking away.

NINE

The sloping grass was cumbersome, making for uneven steps, walking along the service road until Adam reached the intersecting road and the highway beside him continued over a concrete bridge. There were utility poles with power lines that crossed over the highway and traveled in either direction of the street. Beyond the overpass was a long stretch of gray road that disappeared in the distance behind a field of tall grass. Across the street from where he stood were two big rigs with rusted trailers parked in an otherwise empty lot with a white-faded sign and a single wire that hung in a long arch from the sign to an empty building with a FOR LEASE sign on the window. Adam scanned the other side of the road and saw a few stores or buildings. While unable to make them out clearly, he decided to head toward them.

The buildings on either side of the road appeared the same, made with stucco exteriors and large, single-pane windows across the front. Adam was astonished by how open everything appeared as he followed a dirt trail on the grass strip where a sidewalk should've been.

Adam passed a car wash where the partition walls were daubed with patches of off-white squares, concealing the greater part of emblazoned graffiti markings. There were three separate vacuums located in front that appeared broken. One was missing the hose; another was missing the chrome cover, exposing part of the motor inside; the third had a large dent near the bottom from where it might've been dinged by a car. Near the middle vacuum, a plastic trash can endured the weight of several trash bags and an old tire that sat atop the heaping bags. Discarded items formed a separate pile near the bottom of the can in a colorful mess that included crushed soda cans and oily mechanics' rags. Adam looked back at the road, expecting one of the dusty-looking cars that drove by to turn into the car wash, but they just continued past it.

Farther up the road, Adam spotted a building across the street that caught his attention. It looked like every other building he'd passed, but this one had a blue banner strung across the front advertising a chicken fried steak lunch special. Adam realized he hadn't eaten, and he approached the restaurant.

Adam opened the door and stepped inside feeling like he'd entered someone's house, as the restaurant had plush, brown carpet and different style dining tables, each with its own set of unique chairs. Rust-colored spots marked the ceiling, where something had leaked through. The ceiling fans that hung throughout the restaurant were motionless and Adam counted several burned-out lights, giving the room a dull appearance. The walls were mostly bare except for a picture of a classic car and a framed antiquated newspaper article. Adam remained by the entrance, hovering near the quarter machine that offered toys, gum, and stickers.

After a while, he decided to take a seat at a small table near the window.

A woman hurried past Adam, stopped, took a step back, and asked, "Do you need a menu?"

"Yeah," he said, making an effort to smile.

"Okay. Let me just get a Coke and iced tea, and I'll be right back."

"Coke and iced tea, Coke and iced tea," she said to herself as she hurried off.

The only other persons in the restaurant were sitting at two different tables. One table had two ladies and a man; the other had three men, two of whom wore baseball caps.

"I'll be right with you," said the waitress as she flew past Adam, now going in the other direction with the drinks. The waitress came back, flipped a couple pages on her notepad, headed back to a small counter, and returned with a laminated menu. She handed it to Adam, who studied her over before looking at it. Her dark red hair was pulled back to form a ponytail of semi-curled tufts. She was pale, with roseate cheeks and large, sad eyes. Adam expected her to cry, as her expression was marked by shock, or grief, like someone who'd just heard some terrible news. The tight, black t-shirt she wore fit snugly over protruding love handles, and her dark blue jeans had sparkling stones along the contours of the front and back pockets. The look didn't suit her; a person's attire can complement their age, but hardly conceal it.

Adam perused the menu.

"What's the lunch special?" he asked as he reread over the same few items, undecided.

"Chicken fried steak with two sides and a drink," she said, in an almost singsong voice.

"Could I have eggs and hash browns with the special?"

"Yeah. You want them scrambled?"

"Yes, thank you."

"What'll you have to drink, Hun?"

Adam chose coffee. He didn't drink it, but he liked the way it smelled, and suddenly craved some.

The waitress passed Adam a couple more times before she realized she hadn't gotten his coffee. She brought it out, put some napkins on the table, and asked if he needed cream and sugar, but Adam said no. He carefully sipped from the hot cup, then placed it down as he stared at the grain patterns on the surface of the wooden table. Outside, the sun had started to set. Adam could see shadows extending outward from the utility poles and nearby store sign.

The waitress came out carrying a white plate with a blue floral design around the edge. Placing it down with a thud, she pushed the plate over to Adam.

"Enjoy," she said, then ran back to where she came from.

Adam started with the chicken fried steak; it was half the size of the plate. He didn't like the eggs because they were scrambled into tiny little pieces. The coffee had cooled and Adam wanted a soda instead, so he waited for the waitress and didn't touch the rest of his food. As he waited, he realized he wasn't that hungry.

It felt like a long time had passed when she came out and brought the bill, so Adam figured he'd pay and just leave without tipping. While the standard fifteen percent would've been just around a dollar, he wanted to leave a subtle message she'd likely understand.

Adam walked outside, placing his hands along the straps of his backpack, he went in the opposite direction from where he came, passing stores he hadn't seen on his way in.

The ditch on the side of the road had a pipe end sticking out from each side, Adam noticed as he walked by, going against traffic, careful to stay as close to the edge of the road as possible. He looked over, and across the street was a beauty salon next to a Laundromat; both appeared to be closed.

Farther up the road was a new restaurant with a

brightly lit sign and a bright, clean parking lot. There were several cars there which could be seen sitting behind a row of newly planted trees.

The buildings ended, along with last of the empty lots, and there were now thickets of small trees on either side of the road. Adam continued walking, watching the occasional car speed past him in either direction on the two-lane road.

Adam passed some homes. Each was distinctively in need of repair: discolored paints, piecemeal fences, and dirt driveways that pervaded over the lawns. Collectively, they formed a neighborhood that was drab and uninviting. They reminded Adam of his own home, only with more dirt.

For a moment, Adam thought about Michelle without really wanting to. She had always been there for him, willing to talk when something was bothering him, staying up late with Adam on the phone and reminding him that he was an interesting person, wise and funny. He wondered if she'd called him, but quickly dismissed the idea. No, she probably screwed that other guy last night, doing the same things to *that* guy that were exclusively reserved for him, until recently.

She was gone.

The road led Adam past a scrap yard with a sheet-metal building and a high sheet-metal fence. Near the office entrance, a propped-up sign in painted rudimentary letters read, WE BUY PECANS.

Adam passed a small convenience store, paying no attention to it as he traveled in a straight line.

It was nearly dark.

The homes he came across now sat deep within large green lots with rail fences. There was just enough light that he could make out the contours of each home he passed. A few lit, marigold windows stood out sharply against the nightfall.

Minutes later, it was black outside, and all Adam could see were a few lights in the distance that came from a house deep within some open land.

The homes ended and he continued down the road.

Few cars passed at this point. Adam walked, accompanied only by the sound of crickets somewhere behind him and the occasional mosquito buzzing near his ear.

As his eyes adjusted, he could make out a tree line far away. He stared into the horizon and allowed his mind to wonder.

Growing up, Adam had worried about his

parents. Every night, when they thought he was asleep, he lay awake listening through the wall, hearing them clearly as they argued, fearing they would split up. They weren't perfect, but he wanted them to be together. He wanted them to be happy.

Adam's father had a problem; he stayed out late and came home drunk every night. It made him unreliable, irresponsible, and inadvertently, a headache for everyone. Adam hated how he had to grow up witnessing this, and it hurt to face it alone.

His sister wouldn't be spared, and that made matters even worse. Adam knew that everything would somehow be okay, but he didn't want his sister to grow up feeling that this was the way things were supposed to be, that one day she would marry the first guy who would impress her. She'd have children and despise her husband and put up with it for the rest of her life, and in the process lose the compassion to love her own children. Adam had soothed her back to sleep when she was just a little girl, watching all of this. Now she was a teen, and she faced it alone, pretending not to care.

Adam wanted his mommy to be radiant and smiling like the one he thought he remembered from his childhood.

Instead, his mother appeared aged and tired. She had a short temper and was predisposed to fighting. Adam couldn't remember when she had stopped making breakfast on Saturday mornings, and it hurt his feelings a little that she didn't ask if he was hungry when he came home from school. In his heart, he still loved her because he knew it wasn't really her fault. She never imagined her marriage would end up this way, and she was too proud to admit to anyone how miserable she was.

Adam didn't know where he was going, but he couldn't think of a reason to go back.

Stars appeared, scattered throughout the night sky as Adam continued walking. The only thing making a sound now was Adam's footsteps on the side of the road and an occasional sound in the brush nearby.

He hadn't seen a car for over an hour, though he wasn't sure how long it'd been. It was so calm and eerily quiet that Adam imagined what his reaction would be if suddenly he heard a chainsaw being cranked up somewhere in the dark. No, he wouldn't hear anything; the man in the dark would carry a machete, *THUAP!*

Adam heard the hum of wheels on the ground.

He turned around and could see a set of headlights sitting higher than usual and a stream of orange lights of a semi far behind him. Adam made his way toward the center of the road.

He heard it coming closer.

The hum became profound as it turned into a whirring sound.

Adam slowed his pace while watching his feet carefully walk over the painted lines, slower, until he barely moved at all.

The sound was roaring louder, and he could start to see his shadow form against the headlight beams. His mind felt numb. He turned around, made tight fists and, with the flinch of his eyes, a single teardrop rolled down his cheek.

The truck's deafening horn blared.

HOOOOONK!

A flurry of hot air mixed with dirt blew at Adam as he was violently startled. He fell back.

The wheels screeched as the breaks locked, followed by a stuttering sound as the eighteen-wheeler began sliding, swinging the trailer in a long sweeping motion.

Adam rolled over and began crawling on his hands and knees, not watching the truck swerve off the road. He got up and scrambled toward the side of the road as the truck stopped with a deep hiss. Adam breathed deeply. His backpack had fallen off his shoulders, hanging from his elbows as he looked at the truck. He saw a man looking out the passenger window, dumbfounded.

"What are you doing?" the man yelled.

Adam stood paralyzed with fear.

"You crazy son of a bitch. Get off the road!" The driver settled back into his seat and shifted the truck into gear. It maneuvered slowly over dirt and grass, and with a wobbling motion came back onto the road. As it drove away, picking up speed, the truck let out a final honk.

Adam breathed deeply as a long drop of sweat ran down his back. He hung his head in shame. His legs trembled, and he suddenly felt the urge to pee.

The thick grass crunched softly as Adam walked off the road far enough so that if a car passed it would see him, but hopefully not witness the golden stream shooting from between his legs.

He suddenly felt cold and gave a little shiver. Reaching for his backpack on the ground, he pulled out his plaid shirt and put it on. Adam swung the backpack on and continued down the road.

Adam soberly realized what he'd done. *I could have died,* he thought, then swallowed what felt like a large lump in his throat. He pictured his dead body, exploded open, lying at the end of a trail of sanguine streaks. Adam took a deep breath and tried to relax.

For a moment, he wished he was still a kid, when everything seemed simple. Now, walking in the dark along the side of the road, he felt completely exposed and vulnerable. Adam knew that anything could happen and he couldn't just snap his fingers and appear back home.

Adam didn't understand what he expected to see or do as he walked, but the images he saw were breathtaking. A large house that looked like a castle could be seen in the early dawn light.

He walked continuously, passing an expansive green field with just a few trees present. Passing one after another, he walked past several undulating green masses.

A blue pickup passed Adam around the time the sun began to rise. He fixed his attention on the driver's head, which could be seen through the rear window. Beyond the truck, in the distance, large billowy clouds emerged from behind a grassy hill while the golden morning sun nudged its way between the silver-gray masses.

There was a distinct smell in the air.

About twenty minutes later, it became evident what the smell was as he passed a rail fence, and not far behind it were several grazing cows. They paid no attention to Adam. *What a nice life, just eating grass without a care in the world,* Adam thought. *Well, until the part where they turn you into hamburgers.*

Adam cleared his throat, then cupped a hand to his mouth, and with a course voice, let out loudly, "Mooo."

MOOO began one, then another. The brown-and-white spotted cows walked closer to the fence.

Adam continued walking. The grass and trees around him now appeared bright and lively under the light of day.

Wheat and corn grew on the fields surrounding Adam. Farther down, across from him, was a massive field strewn with round bales of hay.

Adam walked, and walked, until he was near a silo and some old machinery surrounded by tall grass.

It was a few more miles before he came across an old sheet-metal building with a dirt road leading to a set of doors. He stopped, walked through the opening on the rail fence, and decided to look inside.

Prying the door open, he could see it was empty except for some chains, a couple rusty tools, and a makeshift wooden table near the back, against a wall. The large sheet-metal door was unwieldy, digging into the dirt. Adam opened it just enough to squeeze through, then closed it the best he could. It was dark and quiet and pervading with dust motes.

Adam slung off his backpack. He plopped down on the dirt floor and kicked off his shoes, then peeled off his damp socks. His feet were sore and hard to the touch, and his toes burned and itched. He began rubbing his feet, scratching, and was immediately annoyed by the putrid smell.

Adam lay back, and for a second, thought of jumping onto the table, but he was too tired. He closed his eyes, took a deep breath, and with his backpack as a pillow, Adam fell asleep.

TEN

Adam awoke uncertain where he was. It was dark, both inside and outside the shed. He lay still, looking into the barely visible mixture of sheet-metal and wood beams that was the ceiling above. Adam cringed as he sat up, wondering if someone had walked in and kicked him repeatedly in his sleep. The soreness was in his shoulders, back, butt, and legs, and he moaned with each movement. He stretched out his arms, rotating his shoulders, then turned and popped his back in a short but loud succession.

Normally, he didn't wake up wishful to be in school, but he had a dream he was late for Mrs. Freud's class. She stood in front of the class giving a lesson while the students asked each other where

Adam might be. He strolled in at the end of the period, still half-asleep and groggy when the bell rang, and Adam woke up. It was a short dream.

Adam's socks were where he'd left them near his feet. He thought he'd packed an extra pair from when he'd planned to spend the night at Michelle's. Adam reached inside his backpack and dug around, feeling for the bundled roll of socks, then got them out. The dirty ones went into his bag, and with a few slaps he dusted his feet, then slipped the clean ones on, careful not to set his feet in the dirt while putting his shoes back on.

Adam stood, dusted his plaid shirt with a couple good flaps before putting it back on, then reached for his backpack. Surprised no one found him sleeping there on the floor of the shed, Adam decided to leave while it was still dark.

Adam pushed the door open just enough to slide out, and headed down the road again. It was early morning but he couldn't tell exactly what time it was. Adam walked along the side of the road, but after a short while he stopped to do a double-take. The field and trees looked strikingly familiar, albeit they were shrouded by the blue-black dawn sky. The same trees with large, sprawling branches, and surrounded by grassy knolls with tufts of flowers and tall plants that he'd seen before. Adam wondered if he was going the right way. The shed was behind him, on the right side of the road, and he remembered it being on his left when he arrived there the day before, so that gave him some confidence he was going in the right direction.

Adam continued walking.

At a distance there was a railroad track.

Adam crossed it, and on the other side there was an intersection. Adam stopped and looked each way, but there was nothing in either direction, so he decided to keep going straight along the road.

The sun began to rise, and by the time it was halfway up, Adam approached another road where he could see a neighborhood far to one side. He figured that's where the school bus he'd seen came from, as one had passed him moments earlier. Adam wondered if to the children inside, he appeared as just a dirty old bum.

Eww, that's your boyfriend, Adam imagined one of them saying. It was the first vehicle he'd seen that morning, and there would be few that would pass him thereafter.

The sun was now bright and warm on his face, and for the next few miles Adam passed a church, a few buildings, and several streets that probably led to more neighborhoods.

The next sound Adam heard was from a random truck turning toward him at an intersection up the road. At the intersection, there were empty fields in every direction. As he walked on, he could see a cornfield with rows of giant, green stalks that came up to the edge of an old two-story house.

Soon after, Adam walked past a sprawling old Victorian home, followed by some smaller, ordinary ones. There was suddenly a sidewalk present, and Adam entered a sleepy little neighborhood, with no people, no cars, no dogs or children playing. Adam paid the homes no attention. He focused on the convenience store ahead where two cars were parked in front.

Adam began groping his pockets as he crossed the parking lot to make sure he hadn't dropped his money when he fell asleep in the shed; it was still there. He stepped inside the cool and dimly lit store and took a deep breath, then let out a sigh of relief as he found himself surrounded by chips, snacks, and every kind of drink he could think of.

There was an elderly man in a plaid shirt paying, and another man with dark hair, wearing a t-shirt, stood in an aisle deciding to buy something. Adam went straight for the fridge and picked out a large bottled sports drink. From the corner of his eye, Adam could sense the cashier watching him. He grabbed a long package of cookies and went to pay. The two items came out to less than five dollars.

Back outside, Adam walked around the building and saw a grass lot with scattered trash and a collection of wrappers that formed a row against the convenience store's wall. At the edge of the neglected lot was an old, rusted metal drum turned on its side. Adam sat on the old drum where he could eat his cookies. They didn't last long. He washed them down with big gulps of his drink, downing half of it in one swill. Adam felt good, and he sat for a moment.

A customer parked near the edge of the building and a car door closed, and Adam sat listening as the person walked toward the convenience store. He wished he could've sat there the rest of the afternoon, and done nothing, but he decided to go and see what was farther down the road.

Adam walked at an easy pace and soon found himself on another quiet farm road. It had turned out to be a beautiful day, warm with blue skies and wisps of pure white clouds.

Off the side of the road was a tractor kicking up

dirt as it chugged along slowly down an unplowed field. Adam watched it make a few passes up and down the field, then he looked up at the sky and wondered about outer space, the moon and how it was close enough to us to affect the tides; the sun and how the light touching his hands was eight minutes old; then he thought about God, somewhere out there in that vast blue sky. How amazing it must be to see everything at once, he mused, and wondered how God must feel when someone prays to Him, asking for something petty, when He's so busy trying to watch everything else. Adam envisioned the trifling things different people at this very moment might be asking for.

'God, please don't let me get hit with a late fee.'

'God, please don't let me fail this class.'

'God, please don't let anyone notice my ugly haircut.'

He then pictured a sickly child from a poverty-stricken country who tried but found it hard to believe in God, because to a child, it wouldn't make sense that a God who exists would allow children to starve.

'God, please don't let my family starve anymore.'

Adam tried not to ask God for anything, because he imagined Him having His hands full all the time. Instead, he believed God gave people brains so they could work their own problems out. He was grateful for that—being smart enough and fortunate enough to care for himself—however, he was glad for that little extra push, that magic when he needed it, that extra set of eyes when no one else was watching—like the truck that could've hit him that night. Was that God?

Adam was enjoying his little adventure. It was exhilarating, wondering where he'd end up next, wondering what might happen along the way—for now anyway. He'd worry about getting home later, so he continued walking.

Adam had read somewhere that the best way to discover a country was on foot. As he experienced that, first-hand, he thought about early explorers that crossed the land and traveled in packs for days without food or water sometimes, and *they* were able to map the terrain and come up with names for the mysterious new lands they encountered. Adam at least had a road to follow . . . until it suddenly ended.

Adam stopped. He stood in the middle of a T where the paved road ended and was intersected by a gravel road. It was quiet. All around him was tall brush and gnarly trees and a set of ruts in the grass that led into the woods. He reached inside his backpack, took his sports drink out, and finished it in smooth gulps. Adam took a few steps over to the side of the road and placed the empty bottle upside-down over a short metal post with a small reflector on top.

Each direction of the gravel road appeared the same, and with nothing to impede his action, Adam decided to follow the ruts in the grass; after all, he *was* exploring. The grass was tall and the sides of the trail were marked by sections of overgrown shrubs that left the path of the rutted road clear and easily ambled.

Adam walked at a steady pace, and every so often, a bug would jump out of the tall grass, startled by the movements of a passerby. Adam later passed a large anthill, and shortly after that there was a rotting log aligned with the rutted road where Adam saw a tiny, white scorpion crawl across the wilted bark.

The rutted road seemed to disappear when it became thick with bushy shrubs and overgrown tress with lacerating branches that were unwieldy, grabbing at Adam as he walked with his arms covering his face. He continued carefully, with his head low, and noticed his shoes were covered in round, prickly stickers; then, to Adam's relief, he crossed a section of shrubs into an open field.

At that point Adam could no longer see the tracks, for the ground there was dense and flat. He kept the sun to his right while he crossed the long stretch of brown-yellow grass. The long field was easy to navigate, even when he realized the sun was no longer overhead.

There was perhaps an hour or less of sunlight and Adam came to the bleak realization that if he became stranded there after sunset, he had no matches, no blanket, and no water. He searched his pockets and his backpack for the lighter he'd bought with the cigarettes, but he must've left it at Doug's. With a sickening feeling, and for the first time since he'd begun this adventure, he started to worry.

Adam considered turning back, but there was nothing back there either, so he might as well go forward. The only thing Adam could think about was another night wandering alone, only this time it would be in the middle of a remote and forested area. His hope was to reach a town and figure things out from there, but things weren't looking well.

The sun loomed even closer to the ground with each minute that passed. Even though he couldn't see it, Adam knew his face was red with sunburn. He touched his parched lips and rubbed his dry eyes, and sighed. As he walked through a coarsely wooded area, he did so with vexation, feeling himself slow down as tiredness crept in.

In the distance, Adam thought he saw something glimmer. He strained his eyes, scanning the horizon as he continued walking. Minutes later he saw a white object that appeared to be a parked truck.

The truck was farther than Adam had anticipated, but he perked up his step in hope of finding someone. Adam was finally close enough that he saw two men standing beside the truck. When he got closer, a third man appeared from behind the truck bed. They talked among themselves in low tones.

"Hi," said Adam, now close enough to ask them for help.

The man standing near the back of the truck was the tallest. He had primed, short hair, a tidy beard, and glasses. He wore a long-sleeved button shirt tucked into his jeans. The shortest one stood behind an open door. He closed the door to reveal a long, black shotgun with the barrel pointed upward. His camouflage hat sat high over his pudgy face, with beady eyes, and a steely, cold stare. The short one spoke first.

"Da' hell you doing walking out here?"

The other two men laughed.

The third man was about Adam's height. He had the stubble of a beard that didn't quite fill in his entire jaw. He had broad shoulders and stood quietly, holding a beer. The stubble man grinned, looking at the other two men while leaning his elbows over the truck's bed.

"I was wondering, can you tell me how to get to town?" Adam asked.

"Well, *which* town?" said the short one.

On opposite sides of the truck, the other two men snickered.

"Which *ever* town is close by," Adam said, getting the short man's attention.

"You getting an attitude with me?" He stared at Adam without flinching, holding the shotgun with both hands.

"Look, I'm lost. I just need to try to get to the nearest town and find somewhere to stay the night," Adam pleaded. He wondered why they were dressed in camouflage and carried shotguns—it wasn't hunting season.

The stubble man dropped his empty beer can into the bed. It clanked around as it settled somewhere in the back of the truck.

"If you take *this* way," said the stubble man. He held an arm out in the direction behind the truck. "Then *that* way." He held an extended arm out in the opposite direction to where the sun had now almost fully disappeared. "You'll find the next town over, but you're looking at about fifteen, or sixteen miles down the main highway."

They chuckled, looking at Adam and back at each other.

The tall man chimed in. "Hell, it's probably about three miles to get to the road. You're looking more like twenty miles."

"Ain't nothing out here but some hogs," Adam heard the stubble man say.

"I wouldn't want to be walking out here, with no damn hogs," said the short one.

There's no way I can walk three miles before dark. Adam did the math in his head; it would be about two hours before he got to the road. There was maybe half an hour of daylight left, but at least he knew which way to go now. Adam had tuned them out, but he heard one say, "Do it, I bet you won't."

The short man stared at Adam and said, "I could take his head off from right here," then smiled. He pumped the shotgun and brought it to his eyesight, aiming it directly at Adam. They burst into laughter. Adam had been in a couple tough situations before, but he'd never been afraid of guns or bullies or anyone who spoke tough or was rough-looking, but there was something about the short man's beady eyes that made him appear evil. Adam stepped aside without saying another word, and walked away. He heard them talking and snickering as he moved farther. Adam heard one clearly say, "Do it!"

A pile of rocks nearby formed a dilapidated wall which stood just a foot off the ground. Adam jumped it, landing on a slump of dirt, then crouched when he heard the sound of the gun blast, shielding himself as a shower of bb's rustled the leaves above, and pelted the ground below. The shotgun cocked again and Adam ran.

Adam's thighs pumped hard, each step sending a painful shock through his legs and up his back. He ran narrowly between two thin trees and jumped a mesh of jutted roots, and with his face grimaced, the sweat drizzled from his forehead.

There was another shot.

Adam didn't bother looking back, afraid they were crazy enough to actually follow him; his instinct told him to keep going. He ran until his chest hurt and his stomach muscles cramped.

Too tired to keep pushing, he slowed down, panting, but continued jogging, feeling he still needed to get away. A fallen tree lay decaying and covered in moss and flat-looking mushrooms, and while Adam should've stopped, he made the push to leap over it instead. He didn't make it. His leg slipped, sending Adam flying. His body turned in a way that he couldn't catch his fall, and he caught a glimpse of the earth below before hitting his head on the ground with a hollow thud.

Darkness fell over Adam's unconscious body. The night creatures flourished and something approached Adam, breathing softly as it came closer.

ELEVEN

Adam slept peacefully. The annoying pressure he felt near his lower back caused him to turn and an arm rested on the pillow lying beside him. He breathed in the sweet smell of fresh lines, then sat up and looked around wildly, unable to see. White smudges blurred his vision. He blinked, turning the white smudges into black blotches, and waited for them to dissipate before looking around. He found himself sitting on the thin, squeaky mattress of a foldout couch. The couch was brown and beige, with various colors that formed stripes on the heavy, woven material. Thin blue sheets with a white floral pattern covered his legs, and as he glanced down, he realized he wasn't wearing a shirt. Directly in front of the couch was an older, box-shaped television with a few pictures mounted on the wall behind it. A narrow wooden bookshelf stood to the left of the television, with only a few inconspicuous paperbacks, some picture frames, and a few decorations. The windows to either side of the television had peach-colored curtains that had been pulled back, and bright light flooded the room.

Adam wondered if he was alone, but there was a distinct sound coming from behind the wall a few feet away. A pot lid clinked, stifling a boiling sound down to a whisper. It was followed by the sound of a spoon being set onto a countertop.

Adam squinted, avoiding the sharp light coming in through the windows. He then rubbed the corners of his eyes, removing the little bits of buildup he could feel, when he heard some footsteps and felt the presence of someone nearby.

Standing in the entrance was a woman of medium hair length, with fair skin, who wore a white long-sleeved shirt tucked into a pair of worn jeans. She turned back, reached for a wooden chair from underneath a table in a dark room, and placed it on the edge of the living room. She sat facing Adam, and leaned forward, staring at him.

"You okay?" she said.

"Where am I?" Adam asked. He pulled the sheets up to his chest and looked over the room one more time.

"You're in my house. You were in my woods last night." She crossed her arms, then leaned back, proceeding to cross her legs.

"I should've called the cops for trespassing," she said, with one leg bouncing over the other. "What were you doing there?"

"I was walking through the forest, trying to get to town, and saw these guys, so I went to talk to them, to ask them for directions. One pulled a gun on me. He might've been playing or trying to scare me, but I wasn't going to chance it, so I ran. He took a shot right over my head. I'm okay, I guess." He reached for his forehead. A sharp pain surged into his head, and Adam groaned. The sensation grew stronger with each second, and he wished he hadn't touched it.

"Yeah, it was red yesterday," she said, about Adam's forehead. "It's black today."

She had a puzzled look on her face, and looked down as she spoke. "It was so weird. You were just sitting there. Taylor found you, so I went to see and, you scared the life out of me. I almost went running back into the house."

Adam watched her, wondering what had happened.

"You got up suddenly, and I mean, I freaked out. You were looking around, like you didn't know which way to go. I kept asking if you were okay, but you never replied. For some reason, I reached for your arm. You walked with me to the house." She uncrossed her legs, and placed her hands in her lap.

Adam stared at her blankly.

"You don't remember?" she asked.

"No."

"You understood everything I was asking you to do. I mean, you even lifted your leg on the steps when I said watch your step. I thought you were on drugs." She shrugged. "I know lots of kids go out to the woods to smoke pot. I find mattresses and old couches out there, and they leave their trash everywhere."

She got up, then came back holding a cup of coffee, staring at Adam as she stood at the doorway, and sipped. "You don't remember, huh? You stood right there, waiting, while I pulled the couch out." She pointed to a place near the door in the dark room.

"The last thing I remember was running through

the woods," Adam said, then scratched his bare arm. "Where's my clothes?"

"You were filthy! You were covered in dirt, leaves, bugs. I had to take your clothes off just so you could lie on my couch. I threw them into the wash this morning. I also have your wallet. I kept your license in case you tried anything," she said before going to place her cup back in the kitchen.

Adam couldn't tell how old she was, but she looked mature, and her voice was soft—unlike the estrogen-induced, high-pitched whine he was used to hearing from Michelle.

"Who are you?" he asked.

She cleared her throat, then her eyes averted as she considered the question.

"Laura." She hesitated a moment before giving Adam her full name. "Laura Lee Garrison. Most people call me Lily."

Laura looked at Adam. She bit her nail, then started to say, "I can't believe I brought you in here. I mean, you could've been hurt, or you could've been crazy." She hooked a fingertip back into her mouth, then took it back out and said, "But the last thing I needed was everyone in town calling me or wondering why there were police cars or an ambulance rushing to my house in the middle of the night. I already have a bad enough reputation as it is."

She turned, walked into the kitchen, then came back out a moment later. "You hungry? I made soup. It's just beef with vegetables, out of the can. That's all there is. I need to get groceries," she said while standing halfway in the kitchen.

Laura took a step toward the living room and looked at Adam. "I've got bread." She held her palms up in gesture.

"I can eat."

A moment later, she brought out a folding tray, and on top was a bowl of soup with a few slices of bread sitting on a napkin to one side. The smell was tantalizing, reminding Adam he was famished.

"Where are you from?" She had sat back down and peered over her coffee mug.

"How do you know I'm not from around here?"

"Besides the fact that I know everyone around here, you don't look like someone from around here." She nursed her mug. "Plus, I looked at your license, remember?"

Adam told her where he was from, but made up a lie about where he was going; instead, he said he'd gone to see a relative. "When the bus broke down, I thought I could walk the rest of the way," he explained.

Adam ate slowly and wondered why she'd helped him.

"Thank you," he said. "That was nice of you to help me."

Adam stuffed a piece of bread into his mouth and slurped his spoon. He stole a glance at the baby picture in a large frame on the end-table next to the couch.

Laura got up, then she returned with a second cup of coffee, though she seemed reluctant to drink it after she sat back down. As Adam ate, she explained with more detail how she was able find him.

Adam looked right at her brown, gazelle eyes as she spoke.

Taylor wasn't her husband, but her blue heeler. He'd been barking for a long time, and she suspected it to be a dead calf or a sheep. Apparently, coyotes drug animals out to the woods and she sometimes had to bury the carcasses. Because she brought Adam in, she couldn't sleep well, so Taylor stayed with her for added protection.

After she finished explaining, Adam looked down and could see the bottom of his bowl. Still hungry, the spoon clinked inside an empty bowl with each deterring scoop.

Laura suddenly got up. "You drink tea?" she asked from the kitchen.

"Sure."

Adam couldn't see Laura from where he sat, but he could hear the sounds of a fridge door open, and a cup being placed on the countertop. A light switch flicked, turning on the fixture hanging over the small round table with four chairs: three adult and one highchair. The fourth chair remained where Laura had left it.

She came back with a glass full of tea, and handed it to Adam. "Sorry, I only have sweet tea."

Adam gulped it down.

Laura stood in front of Adam after she'd gone back for her mug. "I've got to take care of a few things," she said. "It's almost one. I can drive you into town around two or three. Is that okay?" She took Adam's tray, placing her mug on it before she carried it away. "Your clothes should be ready," she said, walking away. "Let me get them."

Laura walked out through what appeared to be the back door and returned later with his clothes folded in her arms, and was followed closely by her dog as she came inside. Taylor came over and lapped Adam's hand. Laura placed his clothes down at the end of the foldout couch. The dog then trotted behind Laura as she went back toward the door.

"You can shower if you'd like. The bathroom is right around the corner." She pointed. "So, an hour?"

"Sure," Adam said. "Thank you."

The backdoor opened so quickly, she probably didn't hear Adam thank her. Taylor shot out and Laura closed the door.

In the quiet living room, Adam heard the screen door outside slam shut as she walked away.

Adam threw the sheets off and lowered his bare feet to the ground. He sat and wondered about the chubby-faced child smiling at him from behind the glass picture-frame. Adam stood and was glad she'd at least left his boxer shorts on. He grabbed his folded clothes, then crossed the living room and saw a small hallway with a wooden floor. To one side of the dark, bare hallway, he could see the bathroom door ajar.

The quaint bathroom had shining white ceramic tile that came up halfway on two side walls and covered most of the wall directly behind the heavy, antique tub with clawed feet. On one side was the toilet with shelves over the top that held a couple of folded bath towels, and on the opposite wall was the sink and mirror.

Adam stepped onto the cool tile floor. Curious to view the damage, he went straight to the mirror where the gruesome image he saw reminded him of something out of a zombie movie. The upper left side of his face bulged, resembling part of a smooth, marbleized plastic ball—a livid purple surface that was tender to the touch.

Adam slid apart the shower curtain and turned on the chrome faucets, letting the warm water mix with the cool as the showerhead roared. He let his boxer shorts fall onto the oval-shaped rug near the tub. He stepped into the tub, then shut the curtain. Mounted to the side of the tub were some plastic trays for holding soap and shampoo. There was a wash rag and a sponge on one of the trays. Adam poked at the sponge as he stood underneath the running water. As he looked down, a stream of dirty water flowed into the drain, and when the water turned clear again, Adam reached for the shampoo and began to wash himself.

After his shower, Adam got dressed.

In the living room, Adam spotted his backpack on the floor beside the couch. He got his toothbrush out and went back to the restroom. By the time he finished brushing, Laura was still somewhere outside.

Adam wanted to do the nice thing and fold the bed back, but when he placed his hands underneath to find the bending spots, the entire thing felt stiff, so he sat on the side he'd slept on and waited instead.

About ten minutes later, she returned.

"Adam, right?" she said, looking right at him.

"Yeah."

"Are you ready?"

Adam looked around, not offering an explanation about the couch or the mess he'd probably left in the restroom, feeling a little embarrassed. "Yeah, I think so."

Laura went across the living room and down the hall to a bedroom, then returned.

"Okay. Well, let's go."

Adam followed her outside. They got into an oversized pickup truck that seemed entirely too large for her. He caught a glimpse of Laura's house which seemed freshly painted in a mocha color with dark brown trim. To one side of the dirt driveway was a horse trailer that apparently had a flat tire. They pulled out of the driveway, and

Adam took one more look at her house and the neat picket fence around her yard as they drove away.

It was a quiet drive for the most part. The area was new to Adam, who looked out the window at rows on a planted field which created an illusion that made them appear to be twirling away as they drove past. There were few homes to see. They passed a deserted, rusted mobile home that had scattered junk around it: a tire rim, an old car door, and some metal barrels that could be seen from the road, despite the weeds and tall grass.

"So, where did you say your *cousin* lived?" Laura asked.

Adam thought for a moment. "I'll just stay at a hotel. They weren't expecting me."

She kept her eyes on the road.

They drove another fifteen minutes and Adam saw a few shops as they entered the intersection that might've been the center of town.

There was an old motel, where Laura pulled into the parking lot. The place looked completely unused, were it not for two cars parked outside, one in front of a room door, and another that sat by itself in one of the parking spots facing the street.

The truck made a half turn in the parking lot, and

Laura parked, leaving the truck on.

"That's the office," she said, pointing. "I think this place is pretty reasonable. But really, it's the only place here, unless you go into the city." Laura surveyed the row of stores across the street. "That barbecue place is okay. And there's a gas station where you could get something halfway decent to eat."

Adam nodded. He undid his seat belt and got down.

"Oh, you *might* need this," she said, handing Adam his wallet.

"Thank you." Adam wished he could've said something showing how grateful he was, but he sensed she was ready to get back to her normal life and didn't seem to be in the mood for small talk.

Adam closed the door and watched Laura drive away. Without bothering to put his wallet back into his pocket, he went over to the office where he spoke through a glass window at the Hispanic woman who sat in a cheap plastic chair and watched a Spanish program on a monitor-sized television. The room she sat in was tiny.

"You needing a room?" the woman asked. She had dark hair rolled into a bun at the top of her head. Her small eyes hid behind puffy cheeks, and she had different sized moles throughout her face.

"Yes."

"You have I.D.?"

Adam showed his license.

She flashed it toward her face, then placed it back through the slot under the glass window. The outside of the office had several long cracks, and flaking paint around the window trim.

"It is thirty-five per night. Check out is at noon," she said. After Adam conceded with a nod, she searched for the key.

Adam paid for one night and went to find his room.

With a squeal, the door opened to a glum room with dark walls that needed a fresh touch of paint. The backboard and nightstand were scuffed, and needed replacing. Adam looked at the carpet and saw tread marks and dark stains that remained after attempts to remove them had failed. He took a deep breath of the stale, damp air, and was glad there was at least a TV, and as a bonus, a small fridge. Getting comfortable wasn't difficult, though. Adam kicked his shoes off and threw his backpack against the wall, then lay on the bed and reached for the remote. They had cable.

The only thing on his mind right now was the

incident from yesterday and how scared he'd been. He thought they were going to shoot him, and he regretted being there at that moment; regretted being so far from home and thought how sad his parents would've been if he'd died out in the woods; died having run away. Luckily, he was okay.

Adam wondered about the woman who saved him. Where was her husband? And her child? Was her husband gone and was she worried he would come home and find a banged-up teenager sleeping on his couch, alone with his beautiful wife? It didn't matter. Adam would spend the night here, relax, and tomorrow, see where the closest bus station was.

A commercial on TV was advertising their Tuesday night movie, and it was one Adam liked. It was about a group of people who follow tornados around, and they're seen as being kind of crazy for getting so close to them, but they're doing it for the sake of helping others. Adam smiled, brought on by a tinge of excitement at pigging out on junk food and watching an exciting movie.

The movie would be on in a half hour. Adam put his shoes back on, made sure he had his cash and the hotel key, and went to the gas station adjacent to the motel.

At the gas station, Adam walked into the convenience store, and passed a man wearing a cutoff t-shirt, one where the cuts came almost to the bottom of the shirt, exposing his flanks and large belly. The man talked to the cashier in a loud voice, telling the cashier what he would do if he won the lottery—promising the cashier he would come back and give him a million dollars. There was a section near the register that showcased some fried food sitting under heat lamps. Adam looked over the limited selection, and asked for a burrito and some chicken strips. A woman came over, handed Adam the food, and jotted something on the paper bags she placed the food in. Adam then got some drinks, chips, and a candy bar. He paid without saying much, then left.

Crumpled bags and wrappers littered the bed and floor of the hotel room as Adam ate and watched TV. He finished one of the sodas and placed the empty bottle on the nightstand where there sat a cheap, plastic phone. Under normal circumstances, a mother would be terribly worried that her son hadn't come home for four days, though Adam pictured his mother, sitting at home and smoking as usual, and while she probably wondered where he was, he couldn't imagine her putting too much thought behind it. Plus, Adam figured he'd go back tomorrow anyway. He decided not to call home. Probably the only person who would be upset by now would be Glen, the store manager at the pharmacy. He would've called every day since Sunday, each time asking for Adam with frustration and despair, as he had no one else who could come in. Adam smiled at the thought. The pharmacy probably closed early yesterday, as he was almost sure he would've been scheduled to work, and Adam was overcome by a profound sense of triumph.

Adam took another shower. The motel restroom was old, but appeared to be clean.

After his shower, he watched more television. Sometime after the Late Show ended, Adam felt his eyes becoming heavy. There was nothing of interest left to watch, so Adam cranked up the AC, turned off the television, and crawled into bed.

TWELVE

There was a booming knock at the door.

It woke Adam, who lay in bed face-down and undressed. He remained there, wondering if the person knocking had the wrong door, and waited to see if they would leave or say something.

"Housekeeping!" came a woman's voice from outside.

The door opened, and a woman in ordinary clothes peeked in. "Oh," she said, then turned away, closing the door as she left.

On the nightstand, beside the cheap plastic phone, was an old digital alarm clock with a faux wood top. Adam glanced over; it was 11:46 a.m.

The air conditioner gushed air loudly, but Adam heard the sheets flap like a sail in the wind, as he pulled them back with a jerk, then he sat up and scanned the room. There were crumpled pieces of trash on the floor, loose change on the TV stand, dirty clothes on the bed and somewhere on the floor of the restroom. There wasn't enough time for Adam to shower and gather his things to be out of there by noon. Adam quickly jumped into his pants. He put his shirt on and slid into his shoes, then stopped to grab his wallet and the motel key.

Even as he rushed through the parking lot, with the sun stinging his eyes, the only thing he desired right now was to continue sleeping. *It's only thirty-five dollars,* he thought, as he made the short walk to the office.

Sitting in the tiny office this time was a younger lady, also with dark hair, who wore it in a bun the way the first one had. She wore no makeup and her glistening face made no expression.

Adam explained that he'd checked in yesterday and wanted the room for one more day. The young lady stared at the side of his face as he spoke, distracted by his bruise that had turned gray with yellow and green swirls. It resembled a spoiled pork chop, last time Adam checked.

She took Adam's money and handed him a printed receipt and some glossy pamphlets which had the names and phone numbers of different restaurants on them.

Using the pamphlets as a visor, Adam went back to his room. He adjusted the AC and threw the pamphlets onto the nightstand before jumping right back into bed.

As he slept, he woke up once or twice, groggily looked around, changed positions, and went back to sleep.

Around 3:30 p.m., Adam lay awake in bed listening to the air conditioner hum in the low lit room and considered the possibility that he may be suffering from melancholia, as he felt unwilling to do anything, but his gloomy bout was broken when he'd become hungry enough that he had to force himself out of bed. He sat up, debilitated by achy muscles, and took a rest on the edge of the bed before standing.

Adam turned on the TV. It was on the news. He stretched, walked around, turned on the light, then jumped back on the bed, landing hard as he sat. From a sideways glance, he noticed the brochures the young lady at the office had given him, and looked them over.

The ads showed colorful pictures of various foods, and promoted the names of several restaurants. The backside displayed events and attractions, and there was even one with a taxi's name and number that would come in handy once Adam was ready to leave. The last piece of literature was actually a folded classifieds just a few sheets long called the *Abilene Star News*. When Adam turned it over, a large ad caught his attention:

$ $ $ $ $ $ $ $ $ $ $

NEEDED

PROFESSIONAL LETTER PAINTER

TOP CASH!!!

CALL ERNEST OF
HALLOWAY HANDYMAN SERVICES
(555-6762)

Adam put the ad aside.

After a quick grooming, he went to the convenience store to find something to eat.

Nothing there seemed particularly appetizing though. Adam chose a sandwich, some chips, and a honey bun. When he paid, seeing the thinning wad of bills made him realize it was probably time to check how much money he had left. Before he turned to leave, he asked the cashier where the nearest bus station was.

"About ten miles away, on the edge of the city," the man told him. Adam thought he could probably walk there.

The town was quaint and moved slow, almost in a dreamlike state. Adam didn't have to wait before crossing the street, and as he looked over at the old buildings in the shopping strip on the other side, he liked their archaic feeling. He thought of the ad and wondered for a moment how much a professional letter painter made; more than a regular painter, he supposed, but then again, he wasn't sure how much a regular one made either. Adam had painted banners and posters for his school, and since he probably didn't have a job back at the pharmacy by now, perhaps that was something he could do . . .

Once he got inside the motel room, Adam ate his sandwich. He didn't turn the TV on; instead he just stared at the ad as he ate. Adam had finished his sandwich, along with the chips, and had tipped back the last of his soda when he decided to call. He picked up the phone and tried the number, and was utterly surprised when someone actually answered.

"Hello?" said a raspy voice.

"Hello. I'm calling about your ad for a letter painter."

"Oh. Yep, need a letter painter."

"I was just curious; how much does it pay?"

"It's for a business I'm painting. I can't believe someone actually called. I'm pretty desperate. We already painted the building, and I need to paint the letters. You available?"

"How much does it pay?"

"Depends on how good you are. I can pay you one hundred dollars. It's not a big area, but I need someone fast. Now, granit, you do a real good job, I'll pay you a little more."

Adam looked down at the soiled carpet, wondering if he should say yes.

"You in the area?" asked the man.

Not sure of the name of the town, Adam explained where he was.

"You know where the Brookshire's in Sweetwater is?"

"No," Adam said. " And I don't have a car."

The man chuckled. "Okay, okay, I drive by that area. You want, I can pick you up in the morning when I drive past there. Will you be at the hotel?"

"Yes." Adam gave him the room number.

"I leave early," the man warned. "Probably be there around six."

"Okay, I'll be ready."

"Mighty fine. I'm fixin' to wrap things up here, and get back home myself."

Adam looked at the digital clock again. It was 4:15 p.m.

"Thanks," Adam said.

"What's your name?" asked the man, who Adam had presumed to be Ernest.

"Adam," he said.

"See you in the mornin', Adam."

They hung up.

Adam was excited about making an extra hundred dollars before going back home. Since he probably wasn't going to leave immediately after the job was done, he went back to the office and paid for the next day. Adam watched TV the rest of the evening and fell asleep around eight.

The alarm sounded at 5 a.m.

Adam woke up, took a shower, got dressed, then ate his honey bun. He washed it down with tap water from the restroom sink, poured into an empty soda bottle.

At ten till six, Adam waited outside, sitting on a short wall near the office.

Ernest showed up in an old model truck with a broken headlight. The paint was dulled and covered in a thick film of sand-colored dust. Two ladders and several extension cords hung from the sides of the truck rack mounted over the bed.

Adam went to open the truck door to introduce himself to Ernest, but struggled with the handle before feeling the door come unlocked.

"How's it going?" Adam said, holding the door open.

"What happened to your face?"

The man sitting behind the wheel had deep, tanned skin with visible creases that formed a pair of ruts over his gray eyebrows. A puffy heap of gray hair matched his beard stubble in a uniform shade of off-white absent of a single indication of his original hair color.

Adam slapped a hand down on the seat as he got in, and a puff of dust rose, residing in his nose and mouth as he sat down. Large tools and pointy objects lined the floor as Adam nestled his feet between the cumbersome objects.

"Wife hit'ya?" Ernest asked as they drove away.

"No, I fell," Adam said. He couldn't help but smile.

Ernest glanced over at Adam as he drove. "Figured that's why you were in a hotel," Ernest said, then added, "without a car . . . because the wife hit'ya."

They made small talk the whole way to the job site, and for the sake of camaraderie Adam agreed with just about everything Ernest said.

Ernest asked Adam if he was hungry, and they stopped for drive-thru.

Adam sipped his coffee and ate, taking the last bite of his breakfast sandwich as they approached the jobsite.

Ernest parked in front of a brick building, then nodded when he saw a person waiting outside.

They got down and approached the skinny man in a baggy shirt with shaggy hair and pointy chin who squatted, waiting near the entrance. The man remained that way until they were close enough, then he stood. Ernest introduced him as JT, and he offered his hand to Adam.

Adam placed his coffee cup on the floor near the building, as he wasn't planning to finish it, and helped Ernest lower some things from the truck.

Once everything was down, Ernest showed

Adam around. They had painted the building and were now laying some laminate down on the floor inside the building. Ernest pointed out where he wanted the lettering done, over an awning, and asked if Adam could do it. Ernest showed him a folded coffee-stained piece of paper with a rough drawing of the letters and how they should go.

"I can do it. But do you have brushes?" asked Adam.

"We have the paint. Tape. Rollers. But I would assume you provide your own brushes." Ernest gave Adam a fixed stare.

"Well, is there a store nearby? I can buy some."

"Yeah. It's not too close, but I need some glue anyhow. You can buy some brushes while we're there."

Ernest left JT with the assignment of wiping off the bare floor while he and Adam would go to the store.

They jumped into the truck and Ernest drove them to a hardware store where they had a decent amount of brushes.

Adam chose several different sizes, and to his surprise, spent a little over $50 there.

Back at the jobsite, Adam collected the things he'd need: his brushes, the paint, a rag, and the scraper that doubled as a paint-can opener Ernest had given him. Adam placed the ladder over the awning and began working.

As cars passed by, they slowed to watch, interested in the newly painted building.

Beads of sweat glistened on Adam's forehead as he painted each letter carefully, concentrating as he pulled down with each stroke, making sure his lines were sharp. With a small brush, he filled in the serifs and stepped down after he finished each letter to see his work from the sidewalk below.

Adam changed colors and painted the second row of letters that were put on faster as they were larger. He finished them off with a white shadow which accented the letters nicely.

Ernest was impressed.

The rest of the morning, Adam helped Ernest and JT put down glue and cut pieces of linoleum.

They stopped for lunch around 1 p.m.

Ernest locked the business door and said he'd be back, then drove away with the window down and a cigarette poking from his mouth.

Adam asked JT if the burger place down the road was any good. It was a small, white building with a picture of a farm windmill on the front.

"Yeah. Big'ol burgers. They're good."

"You want to go?"

"No. Go ahead. I don't eat lunch anyway."

"I'll buy," Adam said.

JT took him up on the offer.

They ordered hamburgers and fries and sat down to eat.

"This is probably my lunch *and* dinner," Adam said, then explained he'd been at the motel for two days.

Adam finished his burger and watched as JT left most of his untouched.

JT got up, asked for a box, then packed his lunch inside it.

"Not hungry?" Adam commented.

"I'm taking it home to my son."

As they walked back, JT told Adam that he lived in a mobile home and he painted for Adam an image of a rough life, one where they were always behind on bills and rent.

Adam wished he could help, but hearing JT talk about his family painfully reminded him of his own.

They neared the jobsite when JT asked, "You work with Ernie before?"

"No. This is my first time."

"Well, just make sure he pays you."

"Huh?"

"Yeah, he pays on Saturdays. Didn't he tell you? Sometimes you have to track him down, though. Especially when he gets to drinking. I've had to go find him at home just so he can pay me. Not that it matters. Shoot, my check's spent before I even get it."

After Ernest returned, the three of them worked until about 4 p.m., and Adam was ready to go.

Not much was said during the drive back. Adam stared out the window the whole time.

Ernest pulled into the motel parking lot where Adam got out, walked over to driver's side of Ernest's truck, and waited.

"Is it okay if I pay you tomorrow?" The large grin on Ernest's tanned face revealed a few missing teeth.

"Well, I have to leave tomorrow. In fact, I have to check out by noon."

"Oh. Yeah, I'll have it before noon. First thing in the morning. I'll drop it off right here."

Adam had no choice but to say okay. Ernest asked about the brushes, but Adam insisted he keep them.

"See you tomorrow!" Ernest yelled out, and the dusty truck drove away.

Adam unlocked his door and walked in. The room had been cleaned, his sheets had been changed, and the trash was picked up. Even his pants had been folded and left on the nightstand, covering the loose change he'd left scattered there. For a moment, he thought the AC was broken as it took him a few minutes to figure out how to turn it back on. Adam set it to cool, then slipped out of his shoes and went to stretch himself out on the noisy bed.

He lay on his side, looking over toward the entrance where the light remained on and created shadows against the TV stand/mini-fridge combo that sat at the foot of the bed. There was some worry, in Adam's mind, that Ernest wouldn't come back in the morning, but he didn't dwell on it too long. Instead, his thoughts changed to Laura. Adam reminisced about the afternoon he'd spent sitting in her living room talking to her, and wished he'd made a better attempt to thank her. At some point, while lying perfectly still, Adam closed his eyes and drifted to sleep.

Adam woke up early, unassisted. He brushed his teeth, took a shower, and made himself ready to leave. He assessed his net worth and noticed he was down to just $27; $27.63, if he included the change.

It was around 8 a.m. when he went to the office and checked out. As he returned the key, Adam checked his pockets, and everything was there, including the classified with Ernest's phone number he'd kept, just in case.

Adam decided to go across the street. He bought a donut and some milk from the convenience store, then went over and waited in the parking lot across from the motel. The small strip of businesses sat higher up, on a slope. Adam decided to wait there, and when or *if* Ernest showed up, Adam could see him coming and simply cross the street and appear less obvious to be loitering than he would from the motel parking lot.

A few hours had passed, and still nothing.

As Adam waited, a white truck pulled into the parking spot in front of him, blocking his view.

The window rolled down. It was Laura. She appeared unusually high up, sitting inside her truck.

Her head stuck out. "You're still here?"

"I'm waiting on someone. I did a job for a guy I just met. He's supposed to pay me today."

"Job? What kind of job?"

"I painted some letters for him."

"Oh, you do that kind of thing?"

"Sort of." Adam noticed her eyes looking to one side.

"How's your head?" she asked.

"Good. It doesn't hurt. Unless I sleep on that side."

"It looks better. A little."

They were both silent as the truck idled.

She smiled and said, "I got groceries, finally." They laughed.

"While you're here, are you hungry? Can I buy you lunch?" Adam motioned toward the barbeque place she'd pointed out when she'd brought him to the motel.

"Thanks. I'd like to, but I have to get these groceries home. But if you want to buy some brisket, we can eat it at my house. The sides are too expensive; I think I have a can of green beans, and corn."

"Uh . . ." Adam hesitated, thinking he should wait.

"I'll bring you right back," she insisted.

Adam agreed, and he was in and out of the barbeque restaurant in a moment's time. With a giant step, Adam climbed in, then shut the large door of the pickup as he plunked down. He set the food in the small space between Laura and himself, then buckled up, looking around the familiar dash once more.

"Thanks, Laura."

"Please, call me Lily. I feel weird when someone calls me Laura because it's usually someone I don't want to see or I owe money to." She snickered. Lily looked back, pulled away from the curb, and rolled down the parking lot, where she turned onto the road.

Adam could smell the food inside her truck and felt his stomach grumble, but ignored them both as he thought long and hard for the right thing to say, having gotten his second chance to thank her. He'd been so scared as he ran into the crowding trees with branches like arms blocking his path, unable to see where he was going and reacting solely to instinct. He knew the men would've done something to him—just another story on the news of a body found in a wooded area, without identification, as they would've taken his money and spent it at a bar, joking about how good of a shot one was while they left that smartass kid to rot.

They were on a farm road surrounded by open

fields with long stretches of tall vegetables stalks. Lily broke the awkward silence by saying, "I thought about you these past couple days."

Adam didn't respond.

"I was worried about you. I even told myself that I could've done more to help you."

"You helped me a lot. You drug me out of the woods in the middle of the night. I don't even know how to thank you."

The rest of the drive, their conversation consisted of mostly small talk, with Lily doing most of the talking. They talked about the weather and how it hadn't rained much lately; the economy and how there weren't enough jobs; and, finally, how there were too many annoying commercials on the radio.

THIRTEEN

Having arrived at the familiar-looking place, Adam was glad to see the outside of Lily's home again, but was also worried he'd miss Ernest. They got out of the truck, and Adam carried the food while Lily carried the grocery bags, insisting she could carry them all herself. They walked through the picket fence, along a light trail in the grass leading to the house.

Lily went up the porch steps and set her groceries down long enough to unlock the front door.

Adam waited with one foot propped on the bottom step, and found himself suddenly up close to her round butt, staring at the worn fabric of her jeans as she bent to pick her groceries back up.

Leading the way was a trail of light from the

open door as they walked in.

Adam stopped to close the door while Lily made her way to the kitchen and set the bags on the counter. Adam met her there, waiting near the doorway, and watched as she put groceries away, moving quickly back and forth while slamming cabinet doors shut.

"Take a seat," she said, motioning her head to the table past the kitchen.

The windows surrounding the dining room let in hazy light that poured onto the wooden table, highlighting its worn center and visible scratches. Adam took a seat beside the highchair and faced the living room. Seeing it from a different angle was like looking into a distant memory—still partially forgotten. As Adam searched his thoughts, still piecing together all the events that led him to Lily's house, he stopped and recognized something in the air. It was the way her house smelled, in that peculiar way houses can have a distinct scent sometimes.

"Do you like green beans?" Lily called out from behind an open cabinet door.

"I like them."

"Okay, we can have green beans, and I've got *these* potatoes." She stepped back from the cabinet holding a box in her hand and looked it over carefully, as if trying to remember how long they'd been in her cabinet.

Lily placed two pots to boil, then walked past the dining table, maneuvering around some displaced chairs, and went to turn on the light. She returned to the kitchen and poured instant potatoes into one pot and the green beans into the other.

"I like putting a beef bouillon cube into my green beans," she said. She stirred the steaming pot with a spoon, then adjusted the temperature on the stove. Lily held the stirring spoon, pointed upward to keep the darkened, soaked end from dripping, and took a few steps toward the side of the table where Adam sat.

"You're only seventeen?" she asked.

"Eighteen," Adam corrected.

The corners of her mouth dented, though the gesture was short of a smile. She turned and went back to the stove.

Adam thought suddenly that perhaps he could let Ernest know he wasn't waiting for him at the motel.

"Mind if I borrow your phone?" he asked.

Lily brought it over, set it on the edge of the dining table, and just as quickly, jumped back into the kitchen.

Adam stood to grab the phone. He reached into his back pocket for the number and called Ernest. When they spoke, Adam explained that he'd left the motel, albeit to Ernest's advantage, it seemed. Ernest explained that it would buy him more time, so they agreed to meet that afternoon. Adam checked with Lily, who said it was okay to give Ernest her address, and repeated it back to Ernest slowly. Ernest would meet Adam there instead.

Adam hung up the phone with the push of a button and it beeped as the lighted buttons went off. He set the phone to one side just in time, for Lily had brought out plates, followed by drinks and napkins, setting everything neatly on the two places across from each other.

Her head moved back and forth, checking to see if everything was on the table before finally sitting down.

The two sat quietly.

Lily looked up at Adam from across the table.

Adam made eye contact with her a couple times, each time finding something in the room to look at instead. "Can I ask you something?" he said.

Lily looked up from her plate. "Sure."

"I was curious. About the highchair . . ." Adam

looked at it, thinking how to phrase his question.

"Oh, that. It belongs to my ex-husband. He has a son. I guess he never came back for it. I just left it there." She took a bite of food, then seemed to say to herself, "But, let's see, that was three years ago. I guess he's four or five by now. I should probably get rid of that thing."

It was quiet for several minutes, and they were nearly finished with their food, when Lily questioned his authenticity. "So, what are you doing out here?"

Adam had one more bite of mashed potatoes left on his plate as he placed the fork down and thought of an answer, one that was true, but he didn't want to say anything too embarrassing or too difficult to explain.

Oh, I come from a pretty messed-up household. See, my parents don't get along. They argue religiously. My father comes home drunk, but tries to make up the next day, then my mom doesn't speak to him, so he comes home drunk, and so on. I left without telling anyone. Then, instead of going back when I had the chance, I spent all my money.

"Looking for work."

"Out here?"

"Yeah."

She frowned, plagued with uncertainty. "Usually, people leave small towns to find jobs." Lily finished her last piece of barbeque-dipped brisket. "What kind of work do you do?"

"Well, I used to work with my dad all the time. He's a contractor. So, I guess I grew up learning to fix things."

"Hm. I have a broken partition in the barn. Maybe you could take a look at it?"

"Sure," Adam said.

Lily cleared the plates, then asked Adam to follow her outside through the door nearest the dining table.

They walked over a wooden porch with a faded surface that creaked as they stepped on the uneven, warped boards. Adam could see a rocking chair and a potted plant to one side. Beyond the porch was a vast breadth of rampant pasture with two small buildings, one on either side. In the distance, long stretches of rail fence marked two different horse pens, and Adam spotted the hindquarters of a light-colored horse, grazing with its back to the fence, whipping its tail sporadically.

Straight back was the sheet-metal building with a large opening on either side where the light shown through. The roof formed a giant A with the eaves coming out several feet to each side.

Lily walked ahead of Adam as he took in the scenery.

"That's where I'd like to keep Red, my horse. I kept a horse there that was too wild. I thought it'd be okay, but he broke the gate." Lily gazed down as she spoke, walking carefully through gangly grass spotted with dandelions and bright yellow flowers.

Adam simply listened, intent on the happenings of equestrian behavior.

"I got rid of him," she said. "But I want to keep Red in there because right now he's just in a large pen by himself. He's pretty old and I can keep a better eye on how much he's eating, if he were by himself."

They approached the lackluster barn and walked inside.

Adam saw the wooden posts and what remained of the wooden gate. There were three stalls, but they were being used for the storage of antique-looking furniture, a rusty old tractor frame without wheels, and square bundles of hay. The partitioning beams between two of the stalls had saddles straddled on top, one behind the other, and on a post, hanging from a single nail, were some oiled reigns.

There were no lights inside, and aside from the natural light coming through the large openings, thin strands of light beamed through the walls where the sections of sheet-metal had gapped apart.

Adam squatted. "Yeah, I can fix that. I have to cut some of it down, so I might need some tools."

"There's some tools," Lily said, pointing at a wooden counter beside the entrance, with a row of cabinets beneath.

Adam pushed himself off the ground. "I'll use these posts and nail or screw some four-by-fours, to fix the dividing wall. Then I can make a door out of two-by-fours." He ran his fingers along the edge of one of the remaining, mangled pieces of wood.

"Oh, if you could fix it, I'd make you a nice dinner."

"It's okay, I owe you. But we'll need wood." Adam looked around the barn, but didn't see what he'd hoped for: a nice pile of lumber. "I might be able to reuse the hinges and the latch, if they come off okay."

"Sure. We can go buy whatever you need. There's a building supplies store about thirty minutes away."

"We could do it tomorrow."

"Okay. I have to work in the afternoon, but if you have to stay and fix it, that's okay."

They went back outside strolling slowly, and Adam saw a big smile on Lily's face.

"I'd be so relieved if that were fixed," she said.

"Is that where they go when the weather is bad?" Adam asked.

"Nah. They just stay outside mostly."

"What happens if it rains?"

"Then they better find a tree."

Adam chuckled.

"I just have to keep Red by himself. Lately, he's been getting kind of thin. My father got him when I was just a little girl. We've had him for over twenty years."

"Wow. I didn't know horses grew to be that old."

"Yeah, he's getting up there. I don't ride him anymore."

From far away, the light-colored horse looked at Lily and Adam as they walked. Its large white and black speckled head followed their movement as the horse stood behind the fence.

The closest Adam had ever been to a horse was once when he had his picture taken on a pony. The white pony had been dressed in a red spangled vest and red cowboy hat, and it had scared Adam, who sat on its back and cried as the photo was taken. He hadn't touched another one since.

They arrived back at the house, and Lily crossed the back porch and reached for the screen door which appeared dated, the wooden contours hidden underneath several coats of paint, and the screen was torn from one corner.

Once inside, Adam peeked over at the stove clock and saw it was 2 p.m. Ernest hadn't showed up. Adam thought about calling him again, but didn't.

"Sit down," Lily said and went to turn on the television.

They sat in the living room and talked about the stories showing on the news. She flipped a few channels and they finally settled on a show about a funny family. Lily laughed heartily, throwing her head back when she did, and Adam watched the television but observed her quietly.

The show ended and she stood, making her way to the kitchen, then returned immediately to the living room.

It was late in the afternoon.

"It's almost time I feed the horses," she said. "I guess that guy never showed up." Lily had gone to the back door, but stopped, and looked directly at Adam. "Do you want me to drop you off after I feed them?"

"Yeah," Adam said, sounding unsure. He knew he didn't have enough money for another night at the motel—he didn't have any money at all. *I'll figure it out,* he thought. "That's fine."

Lily stepped outside.

Adam got up, found the phone, and dialed Ernest's number. It rang, but eventually the call reached his voicemail. *I could just wander around there and call him at night—I don't know.*

After a while, Lily came back inside wearing a large, pearly white smile.

"Would it be okay if I crashed here?" Adam asked abruptly.

Her smile vanished. She pondered the question, her eyes searching the room while she thought. Finally, she said, "Okay. Since you'll fix my stable tomorrow anyway, right?"

"Yes." Adam smiled. "And it gives Ernest more time."

"Oh, okay. Well, I wasn't expecting to have someone for dinner, so I guess I should get started on it." She wiped her hands on the seat of her jeans and went into the kitchen where the lights came on, leaving the soft orange glow to spill into the far end of the living room.

Adam was resting on the couch when Lily came over and asked if he liked chicken and gravy, and when Adam said yes, she went back to cooking.

"Is it okay if I give Taylor some of the leftover brisket?" she asked, peeking around a wall.

"Sure. I don't mind. Where is he, anyway?"

Lily disappeared and spoke from behind the wall. Her voice sounded muffled, but Adam could make out her words well enough. "I don't know. He goes out to the neighbors' houses sometimes. He just comes and goes, but he's usually here by dark."

Lily remained busy in the kitchen and Adam could smell the tantalizing emission of a baked bounty.

Lily stood facing Adam, near the living room entrance. "Just five more minutes," she said.

She snapped her fingers and walked past him, then rummaged through a medicine cabinet or a drawer in the restroom.

In the hallway, she called to Adam. "Come here a sec."

Adam stood and walked around the couch. She was holding a small white jar. Adam stooped forward when Lily asked him to come closer.

She rubbed his tenderized face with a soothing

cream that tingled Adam's nose and made his eyes water. The lid clasped back onto the container, and Lily walked back to the restroom.

She came back out. "There," she said. "Does that feel better?"

"What is that stuff?"

"It's an ointment. My parents used it on me all time. I was always falling or hurting myself as a kid."

Lily went back to the kitchen where she would serve their plates, and Adam took a seat at the dining table.

While they ate, Lily talked about how empty the shelves at the grocery store had been and how long it took to check out, to her surprise. She preferred the grocery store over Wal-Mart on the premise that shopping at Wal-Mart usually became an all-day event. She then explained that she worked at a small restaurant in the evenings that was frequented by many of the locals. Lily usually had two nights off per week and tonight was one of them. It was where she'd learned the recipe to the gravy Adam had sopped up with several of the buttered rolls.

Afterwards, Lily picked up the dishes and washed them, wiped the table and the kitchen counters, then finally joined Adam in the living room where they watched an old action movie; Adam had seen it, but it was new to Lily.

Halfway through the movie, Lily popped popcorn, then sat on the floor where she shared it with Adam.

There was a sound at the back door.

Lily stood. When she opened the door, Taylor came rushing in, wagging his tail, and threw his paws on Adam's chest, knocking him onto the floor.

"Heel!" Lily said.

Taylor looked over at her with his tongue lolled, but didn't budge.

"Down!" Lily pulled at his collar. "I teach him not to do that but I guess he's just excited." She pulled him off Adam, and walked him to the back door. "I don't have many visitors, sorry."

She fed Taylor outside, then sat back down on the couch opposite Adam.

Lily remained on the couch a short while, then stood and announced, "I'm going to get ready for bed." Before leaving, she reached for one of the couch cushions and propped it up on the corner where she'd sat.

Adam got up and moved to one side as Lily bent

down to unfold the couch in a springy clang. She left, then returned with some linens and a pillow. Lily tossed the pillow to one side and pulled the fitted sheet around the corners of the foam mattress, then spread the flat sheet out, and smoothed it with her palms.

She turned off the TV before leaving the room again.

Adam found his backpack, searched for his toothbrush, and went to the restroom, arriving just as Lily walked out. They grazed each other in the narrow hallway. Adam glanced at the two pointed nipples poking out from under her pajama top. The shorts she wore were small and exposed her creamy looking legs.

"Oops," she said.

Adam thought he saw her smiling.

He stood in front of the vanity and brushed his teeth, looking at the bruise in his reflection that seemed to look a little better. Adam went back to the living room where he crawled under the fresh-smelling sheets, and lay on the foldout couch breathing in the scent of the linens mixed with the astringent ointment. The house was deadly quiet when Lily suddenly peeked around the wall.

"Good night," she said. Her hand reached over

and turned out the living room light.

Lily's bedroom door closed and the lock turned with an audible click.

Adam realized he hadn't seen Taylor come back inside, and just then he heard him whimpering outside.

Lying in the dark, Adam rested easy, relieved that *he* didn't have to sleep outside. *Maybe she'll pay me something for fixing the stable, then I can go home, finally.* With a deep breath, he dozed off.

The sun was up, and Adam lay asleep when someone at the door knocked.

Adam woke up and looked around, but didn't see anyone. He got up and walked through the kitchen toward the formal living room at the front of the house where he thought he heard the tapping.

The windows in the center of the living room didn't give a good view of the front door, Adam noticed with a failed attempt at trying to see through the veil curtains. They fell back in place as he let them down. He had no choice but to check who was there.

Ernest stood at the door. "Hey, didn't make it yesterday. I had to go across town," he said. Ernest held up some money. It was $130. The bills were folded in his hand and he held them out, handing them to Adam. "I paid you a little extra. I appreciate you helpin'."

"Thanks."

"You want to help me with another job? JT quit on me—guess he found himself a real job." Ernest grinned. "I'm busier than a dog with two peters," he said, wiping his brow in gesture.

"Just today?"

"No. It's another town over. It's pretty far. I'll stay in a hotel there for a week. I'll pay the room and I'll give you $150 a day for five or six days. I only paid JT 'bout half that because half the time he was drunk or high and didn't show up on time."

"Can you wait here just a minute?"

"Sure." Ernest stood on the front porch, scratching his stubbly beard.

Adam shut the door. He hurried to the living room where he'd left his shoes, and slipped into them. Frantically, he checked the house, then dashed outside.

Lily wasn't in the yard, so he ran to the stable. There she was, hunkered down, surrounded by various tools strewn around her.

She stood. "Is everything okay?"

"That guy who was supposed to come by . . ." he said, catching his breath. "Well, he just showed up. He paid me, but he wants me to go with him for a week." Adam studied her face. "Would you mind if I came back in a week? I'll fix your stable, I promise."

"Sure. No, that's fine." Lily looked down at the clutter around her feet from where she'd been searching through the cabinets in the stable.

"Okay." Adam stood waiting for a moment. "Thanks for letting me spend the night. I owe you big time. I have to leave now, but I'll see you in a few days, okay?"

"It's okay."

"Bye," Adam said.

"Bye," she said to Adam, who'd already turned around and was headed for the house.

Adam quickly gathered his things and left.

FOURTEEN

Ernest surprised Adam when he picked out a nice hotel for them to stay in. They checked into a single room with two large beds that sat directly across from each other, complete with contemporary art and sleek furniture.

Over the course of their stay, Adam witnessed an unflattering side to Ernest. He smacked his mouth as he ate, and burped from deep within the pit of his stomach, a sound strong enough that Adam was sure could be heard from outside their small room. At one point Ernest lay in bed with his tanned, stubby finger buried deep inside his nose, and when he'd felt confident with his findings, pulled it out and wiped it on the pillow beside his head. The smells were bad too, alternating by orientation and potency.

Despite lacking manners, he did have a good work ethic and prompted Adam to sleep early so they may rise early as well. By 6 a.m. Adam could be found in the lobby, making use of the breakfast bar, and by 6:15 they were usually gone. Ernest waited in his truck, smoking a cigarette and scratching a lottery ticket, and although he skipped breakfast, he did drink coffee, and was apt to do all three things simultaneously while he drove.

Each morning, they arrived at the jobsite by 7 a.m. and worked until noon or one, usually finishing for the day by 3 p.m.

At night, Ernest sat on the hotel patio, smoking cigarettes.

Adam asked him once if he was married.

"Oh yeah," Ernest said. "Being married is like winning the lotto—sometimes you gotta try a few times before you get lucky."

Adam felt like a natural working with tools and lumber. He couldn't remember liking it before, but he liked it now that he wasn't under his father's constant scrutiny. Adam cut pieces of plywood, always careful to mark the 'cut' side, and brought Ernest a piece of wood that installed perfectly. Everything Ernest asked him to do, Adam executed beautifully. He cut sheetrock, applied the tape and bedding, and he could texture and paint. Adam worked proudly and kept the jobsite tidy. He even changed the power cord on a reciprocating saw, which seemed to excite Ernest profoundly.

The week flew by, and by Friday, they had finished.

Ernest explained to Adam that he didn't work more than he had to, and in upholding his philosophy, they stayed one more night at the hotel.

Early the next morning, Ernest cashed his check, then paid Adam in hundred-dollar bills. Adam counted it several times, impressed by the amount of money he'd made in such a short time. Impressively, he'd spent about $20 on food throughout the week and now had over $800.

Ernest refused to check out before noon, so at fifteen after twelve, they headed back.

The long drive was quiet and smooth enough that Adam nodded off with his arm resting over the open window of the truck, and with the warm sun gilding his face.

He opened his eyes and looked around groggily. They were on the road leading to Lily's house.

"Did ya fall asleep?" said Ernest.

"Yeah. I guess I was a little tired."

"We're almost to your house."

Adam hadn't explained that he was merely a visitor, and there was no sense in trying now. Once they were close enough, he spotted Lily's truck sitting in the driveway and took it as a good sign.

"Man, I should take back twenty dollars for gas money—driving out here," Ernest said. The drive took about an hour, and Ernest still had a farther drive to his house.

Ernest pulled up behind Lily's truck.

Adam thanked him, and they shook hands.

"I appreciate ya," Ernest said before he backed out of the driveway and headed down the road.

Adam saw the drivers' side door of Lily's truck open wide. She sat inside, looking at him, and slid down.

"You're back!" Lily walked right up to Adam, close enough that he could see directly into her liquid brown eyes. She'd cut her hair short, and it was now a copper-red color. For the first time, Adam noticed, she wore makeup and had on lipstick.

"I just got in," she said, and started for the house.

Adam stood behind Lily, waiting for her to unlock the front door. She spoke as she turned the key. "Are you fixin' my stable today?"

"Yes. I'll start on it right now."

They entered the dim, quiet house, and Lily quickly went to turn on some lights.

"What was it you said you needed again?" she asked, standing in the kitchen. "I can go to the store and get what you need."

"Let me see. Can I go back there to check out your tools?"

"Of course. Go right ahead."

Adam walked outside through the back door, and in the distance he saw a ball of black and white fur hurling toward him. Taylor jumped through the rail fence and caught up to Adam, where he pounced onto his chest.

"Hey," Adam said, taking hold of Taylor's paws. "Let me go to the barn. I need to fix something." He let Taylor down, who obediently followed.

Adam had a puppy once; he remembered it vaguely. Its name was Butch, or Bruno, or something equally conventional, but it didn't live long. He found it lying dead in the yard one morning, and although he was just five or six at the time, Adam understood that taking the dog to the vet would've been out of the question, if there were ever a chance of saving him in the first place.

Spending money on pets wasn't tolerated, not so much as even buying dog food. Adam's father had balked at the price of it when they'd first gotten the puppy—*that* image was still clear in Adam's mind. Perhaps he could get one once he returned home.

Adam went inside the barn and searched the cabinets he'd seen Lily dig through. Taylor froze, then lowered his head, curiously sniffing each item Adam took out. There wasn't much there: an old, rusty handsaw, a couple of hammers, a wrench set, more or less, a palm sander, and a few random screwdrivers. Adam pulled cobwebs off some of the tools, and dusted the ones he set aside.

"Adam?" Lily called as she approached the barn.

Taylor became excited and began lapping the corner of Adam's face, from where he'd already begun to sweat.

"Stop it, Taylor!" she said, sounding stern but wanting to laugh at the same time. "I'll get him out of your way." She went for his collar, but Adam said it was okay.

"Do you have a lamp?" he asked, and looked up at the dark corners of barn. Cutting wood inside would be a challenge, if not dangerous.

"I have one in my bedroom," she offered.

"No, they have some you can use when working.

They have a small cage, and you can hang them from the wall. I'll get one from the store."

"Oh, you want to go with me?"

"Yeah." Adam studied the damage one more time and made a mental note of what he'd need. "There might be something else I need that I can't think of right now."

"Okay."

As they were leaving the barn, Lily placed a hand on Adam's arm and asked, "Have you eaten yet? Do you want to eat something before we leave?"

"I'm fine," Adam said, ready to work.

They went through the house where she grabbed a leather hand purse and her keys and they headed for the building supplies store.

The warm day was made pleasant by a gusty breeze, while the trees they passed alongside the road waved their branches in rhythmic sequence.

Lily lowered her windows and sang energetically to a loud tune playing on the radio. It didn't bother her that she was being watched, holding a fixed smile on her face.

A short drive later, they arrived at the store, where the only vehicles present were pickups scattered throughout the giant parking lot. Lily came in at an angle, parking without regarding the lines, and killed the engine.

Adam got down and waited for Lily, then they went inside. The smell of plant products and lumber summoned up fragile memories for Adam, considering one of the only places his father had taken him to as a child was a similar store.

Adam pushed a rattling flatbed cart with ease, and went directly for the things he'd need. Lily followed him without question. In the tools section, Adam found a cheap circular saw and a new drill. Then he crossed off a few more things from his mental list: a new tape measure, screws, and lumber. All that was left were a couple extension cords and the lamp, and he picked up a tube of carpenters' pencils as well.

With everything he needed on the cart, Adam looked at Lily and said, "That's it."

They went to pay, and Lily's face appeared worried as she watched each item being scanned, but Adam had taken his wallet out and removed a few bills from one of the folds.

"No," she said, trying to stop him.

"It's okay. I owe you." Adam paid, and the cashier handed back his change with a long, curled receipt, and said something about a survey, which Adam disregarded.

Lily thanked him and they walked out to her truck with Adam pushing the noisy cart.

On the way back, she asked again if he was hungry, but Adam preferred to finish the job at hand and eat later, and she understood.

Back at Lily's house, Adam got the tools down and took them out of their boxes. He plugged in the extension cords and ran them from the house to the barn. Lily helped bring down some of the wood and she brushed her hands off after she set the boards down.

She stood outside the barn, looking in at Adam, who finished opening packages.

"Well, I wasn't sure when you'd come back, so I don't have anything to cook. I'll run and grab a few things while you do that."

"Okay."

"Now, I said I'd make you a nice dinner. I don't know how to make a lot of things, but tell me what you like and I'll try to make it."

"I don't care."

"No, pick something."

"I'm not picky, really. Pick something *you* want to make."

"Well, I haven't had meatloaf in a long time. I make potatoes and mixed vegetables with it. Do you like that?"

"Sure."

"No, seriously, do you like meatloaf?"

"I've never had it."

"You've never had meatloaf?" She narrowed her stare at Adam, and a small wrinkle formed between her brows. "Where did you say you were from?"

Adam laughed. "My mom never made that, sorry. But I'd like to try it."

She smiled. "Okay. I'll make it. Can I get you anything while I'm at the store?" She looked Adam up and down.

"No, thanks." Adam plugged in the lamp. "I'm fine." The light from the lamp created a cavernous, incandescent effect and Adam took a moment to look around for one of the hammers he'd seen earlier.

"I'll be back," Adam heard Lily say as she walked away.

One of the pieces of wood jutted up with a splintered end. Adam placed a hand on it and gave it a good whack with the hammer. After he removed a few more pieces, he continued working, marking the wood and cutting boards and placing wood beams where the old ones had been knocked off.

Adam constructed a door like his father had taught him once when they built a fence together. He remembered how sore he'd been, digging holes by himself with a two-man auger while his father worked closely behind, mixing concrete and setting posts. The door frame was a basic square with one beam that crossed it diagonally, like a Z. Adam recycled the pickets, and was able to reuse the hinges and the hasp, fitting everything so it opened and closed easily.

It was hot and stuffy inside the barn. Adam walked through the opening where he could get some fresh air.

Taylor trotted over and licked Adam's palm, wanting to play as he jumped back and barked.

"What is it?" Adam said joyfully.

The dog barked again, then ran away, flitting across the grass field as he made his way toward the side of the house.

Adam had decided to do a few finishing touches, when Taylor came back with a ball in his mouth and pushed it against Adam's leg, letting it fall. Taylor barked again and waited with his tail raised as it wagged in anticipation.

The ball was smothered with slobber and gritty

dirt. Adam launched it as far as he could and watched Taylor run as if his life depended on the retrieval of that green orb. With the ball in his mouth, he headed back toward Adam, but let it go in pursuit of another venture. Taylor chomped at a butterfly, but its unpredictable movements secured its safe passage.

Adam turned to go inside, seeking out a couple more tools, and when he looked up, Lily stood at the entrance.

"Oh, wow, I can't believe you're done already." She looked over at the bright pieces of unfinished wood worked in with the gray decrepit pieces. Her hand tried the hasp and she opened and closed the door. "Nice. I can't thank you enough. I didn't ask, but how much do I owe you?"

"Nothing. You helped me out, so it's the least I can do."

She looked over at Adam as he picked out a hammer and a large file.

"A couple screws are poking out a bit," Adam told her. "I'll file them down so no one gets hurt."

"Thank you," she said. "Well, I'm going to get dinner ready, so I hope you're hungry."

Lily walked away and Adam finished smoothing out some of the protruding screws and rough ends.

* * *

It was late in the afternoon—around five or six, Adam suspected—when he had all but finished putting away the tools. The new tools, along with the old ones, went into the cabinets Lily used for tool storage. Adam couldn't see himself boarding a bus with a circular saw, and it was an inexpensive model; plus, he didn't want it.

Taylor lay in the tall grass and watched Adam coil the extension cords around his crooked arm, wrapping it around his elbow and open palm. The coiled extension cords fell with a thud on the porch, and Adam walked inside.

The house smelled like seasoning and steamed vegetables. Sounds blared from the TV in the living room. Lily came out of her bedroom and crossed the living room, headed for Adam.

"All set?" she said, standing in front of Adam.

"Yes." Adam took a deep breath.

She looked at Adam's dirty clothes. "Do you want to take a shower before supper?"

Adam wanted to just sit down and eat; he felt hungry and tired now. However, standing there, his hand reached up to scratch his head when he caught a whiff of his manliness and changed his mind, agreeing to shower.

"Do you need some clothes?" Lily asked. "I have some old shorts and t-shirts that belonged to my ex-husband. They might fit you."

Adam realized he hadn't washed clothes the week he'd spent with Ernest. "Okay, I'll try them on."

Lily disappeared. Adam heard a dresser drawer snap and she returned with a pair of swimming trunks with the knit underwear inside and a pocket tee. The clothes smelled fresh, comparable to the way the house smelled earlier.

"Are you staying the night?" she asked after handing Adam the clothing.

"If that's okay with you?" Adam's response sounded natural, even though he'd been caught off guard by the question. As tired as he was, it sounded like a good idea.

"I don't mind. Is there anything you want me to wash?"

Adam looked down at his sawdust-ridden clothing.

"Just bring me your clothes when you get out of the shower," she said.

Adam took a quick shower with warm, strong water that pelted down in a singing manner on

Adam's back, unlike the shower at the hotel that had sprayed a languid stream.

The clothes fit a little loose, but at least they were clean. As he dressed, Adam rubbed the lower part of his stomach where his fat bulge used to be. He shook off his dirty clothes and brought them to the living room.

"Just set them on the couch," Lily said.

Adam sat at the table. A moment later, Lily set down a loaded plate of food in front of him, with steam lifting off the top, and it struck Adam as amusing.

"I can't believe you've never had meatloaf." She brought over her plate and sat across from him. "My mother used to make it all the time. She hated it, but me and Daddy liked it, so she would make it for us—the poor thing."

Ready to try the thick slice of meatloaf with a layer of glistening ketchup to one side, Adam reached for the salt shaker and shook it twice: once over the vegetables, once over the roasted potatoes.

"Do you want bread?" Lily asked and had begun to get out of her chair.

"No. This is fine."

Adam watched Lily cut into her meatloaf with her fork and place a bite of food carefully into her mouth. While they ate, Lily talked, mostly. Adam had learned from Michelle that sometimes women wanted to talk and they only wanted someone to listen while consenting not to judge them.

She spoke trifling about the things that happened the week he was gone: the funny things she'd watched on television; her trip to the store and how she got mad at a slow cashier; her visit to the beauty salon and that she thought it was silly when women got their nails done all the time.

"They look nice." Adam remembered she had gotten a haircut too, and thought to comment on it. "You look pretty."

Lily smiled. "Why, thank you."

After dinner, Lily sent Adam to the living room while she stayed to clean up.

Even after a shower, Adam felt hot and muggy. He realized the air conditioner hadn't been on, and the warm air made him feel sleepy as he sat there, watching television.

Lily came out and sat one space over on the couch. She seemed to reach for Adam's leg, her fingers brushing his thigh as she reached for the remote instead.

"Is there something you want to watch?" she asked.

"Anything is fine."

They channel surfed for a while until a program about rainforests caught their attention.

Around ten, Lily said she would get ready for bed and Adam watched the rest of the show. She came out fifteen minutes later and stood at the living room entrance in a flower patterned nightgown with a ruffle trim around the low-lying neck.

Adam stood, and waited for her to pull the couch out, but she remained there, fidgeting her hands, and staring off into the side of the room.

She walked up to Adam, put her hands on his shoulders, then leaned in and kissed him softly on his neck. Adam's palms were sweaty, being the room was so warm, and he stood there worried she'd notice, then he closed his eyes, letting her soft lips travel upward. As she reached his ear, he swelled up in his shorts, feeling himself uncomfortably press against the knitted underwear. Adam turned to look at her, seeing the moss green hue around the center of her eyes, then he kissed her on the lips, tenderly feeling them with his until everything he knew escaped his mind like a great void. They kissed passionately. Adam put his hands around her waist, feeling the curves of her body through the soft nightgown, and dug his fingers into the supple yet delicate surface.

Adam stopped. "Are you sure we should . . ."

Lily pulled Adam toward her, walking backwards until she sunk into the couch and let him rest between her legs. She put her hands under his shirt and peeled it off, then kissed him on the chest. Their eyes met as she dug two thumbs into the sides of his shorts and pulled them down, where they fell to the floor.

Lily stretched herself out and closed her eyes as she laid back.

Adam lifted her gown, exposing her smooth legs, and noticed there was nothing underneath. That was the last thing he saw, a neat patch of hair, before he eased inside. She wrapped her soft legs around Adam's back, and he felt her moisten as he began to move gently but with a desire for intensity.

Lily moaned and tossed her head back, gripping Adam's arms and squeezing her thighs as he moved.

Adam didn't last long, as he'd been too excited, and failed to bring her any real pleasure. Lily stood and turned the television off, then asked Adam to come to her bedroom.

A desolate ceiling light let out a faint yellow glow, creating shadows on the sides of the velvety red curtains that draped to the floor. The farthest window had an AC unit that filled the room with comforting cool air. Against the wall was a rustic wooden dresser covered in perfume bottles and cream jars.

The bed had several pillows. Lily walked over and removed some of them, leaving only two, then pulled back the sheets. She walked around the bed and clicked on an old lamp that sat on a nightstand before going to turn off the bedroom light.

"Lie down," she said to Adam, who stood in the middle of the room.

Adam lay on the cool sheets and felt his head sink into the cushy pillow.

Lily turned off the lamp, and in the pitch black room, she slid into bed, pulling the sheets around until she got comfortable. She faced Adam and moved closer, placing her hand on his chest, and stroked it sensually.

"I feel bad," Adam admitted.

She stopped stroking him. "Why?"

"Well, because I didn't last long."

Lily shushed him. "You must be tired," she

whispered, then pulled the blanket up so they were both covered.

Adam breathed quietly, containing his excitement as he pictured her lying there. He lay awake until his eyes adjusted and he could see Lily's silhouette in the dark.

The room glowed with the soft light from the rays of the mid-morning sun. Adam heard a sound, like a door close as he lay in bed alone. He looked around, wondering if he'd been dreaming, but the memories felt too real. The images of her naked body were still fresh in Adam's mind, and he felt himself become aroused thinking about her.

Last night, the very moment he went inside, he knew he wanted to do it to her over and over again and nothing else in life mattered. Adam was still fantasizing when she opened the door.

"Good morning," she said, standing in the doorway. "I'm usually up pretty early, but I was trying not to wake you. Are you hungry?"

Adam rolled to one side, making no sudden movements as his back muscles were achy from working in the barn. Lily walked in and placed something on her dresser. She wore stiff-looking blue jeans, with stitched W's on the back pockets and a white blouse where underneath were the prominent dark lines of her bra straps.

She turned toward Adam and stood close enough that he could grab her, but resisted.

"I had coffee earlier," she said. "There's still some in the pot. Do you want some?"

"Sure."

Lily walked away, and Adam followed her into the kitchen. She carefully handed Adam the mug, and he held it, letting it cool. After looking through one of the cabinets, she asked Adam if he liked oatmeal. Adam politely said yes, grateful that she'd been so kind and caring to him. The way he felt right now, she could've offered Adam a cardboard paper towel tube and he would've eaten it, because it came from her.

"Take a seat." Lily parted a grapefruit in two. She kept one half and brought Adam the other, along with a bowl of plain oatmeal and a glass of milk. She pushed a chair over so it was closer to Adam, but went back as she'd forgotten something, maybe a spoon.

Adam sipped his coffee while he waited for her. The coffee wasn't like the stuff he'd had before; it was actually good. The oatmeal was thick and bland, so he only tried a couple spoonfuls before moving on to the grapefruit. He watched Lily, who pulled up chunks of grapefruit with her spoon, so Adam stabbed it with his and, as if for the sole purpose of her amusement, a blinding shot of grapefruit juice shot Adam in the eyes. Lily let out a spell of laughter, but stood, and brought Adam a dampened dish cloth.

"I'm sorry," she said, giggling. "Don't hold it up like that. You start from the outside, near the skin." She ripped out a mushy spoonful and popped it into her mouth. "Like this."

Adam ate another spoonful of oatmeal, remembered he hadn't liked it, then commenced to peeling his grapefruit like an orange.

After the dishes were put away, they simply talked. Lily asked most of the questions and Adam answered as best he could. Having realized he could make her laugh, Adam wanted to watch her do so again, but couldn't think of something funny to say. The conversation eventually led to the outcome of their afternoon as she explained that she would have to work.

It was around one o'clock when she made sandwiches for lunch, then got ready to leave; she would go in at two.

Lily had gotten her keys and was standing close

to Adam before she left. The soft breasts under her blouse pressed against his chest and Adam tingled all over.

"I'll be home around 9 o'clock," she told him. "Are you going to be here when I get back?"

Adam smiled and said yes—he couldn't wait. She kissed him and bit his lower lip gently as she pulled away.

Lily rushed out the door and left.

He couldn't believe she would be with him again—tonight, alone, in her house—but for now, he thought, what to do for the rest of the afternoon?

First, Adam sought out his clean clothes and decided to take a shower. The warm water felt like a thousand tiny hands massaging his back, a therapeutic sensation so relaxing, Adam reminded himself that some things need not rushing.

He put his clothes on, then walked down the dark hallway leading into the formal living room. At first, Adam had no intentions of snooping, but as he glanced around the old house, it appeared all the more peculiar.

The windows on the foremost wall were being fed by vigorous beams of light, while the light from one window veered as it touched a glass ornament, projecting a broken nimbus of squiggles and dabs onto the dark green walls. There were photos on the wall that appeared to be Lily when she was younger, and her parents. One was of a man clad in a button shirt and a cowboy hat, with one hand hooked onto his belt and the other over Lily's shoulder. She wore a shirt with an embroidered collar and a similar hat to her father's. The red-tinged photo next to it was blurry but discernible: a young man with short hair and a mustache, and a young woman with bouffant hair and heavy blush.

Amid a long wall, there was a stone hearth fireplace blackened inside from use, and near it was a moose head sitting on the floor. A burly buck with divergent antlers like wooden spoons, it had a broad neck which served as a sitting stump, and it stared at Adam with menacing eyes. Adam circled the furniture: one sofa and one loveseat, both elegantly crafted in curved frames with cabriole legs.

In a corner by itself was the front door and straight across from it was the kitchen entrance. Adam passed through the kitchen, heading into the living room, with its softer colors.

The couch conformed to the contours of Adam's body as he lay there, with his mind lost deep in thought. He couldn't stop thinking about Lily and waited there until she came home, without so much as turning on the television.

Adam heard the sound of her keys jingle as she walked in, and he could also hear some bags. Lily had brought home food from her restaurant, but since Adam just lounged around all day, he wasn't hungry.

After she settled in, they watched TV, holding hands as they sat close together on the couch. Not long after, they became lip-locked and went to make love.

It was better the second time, and when they finished, Lily said loudly, "I came?" She sounded both surprised and relieved.

They lay beside each other and Adam looked at her curiously.

"Oh my gosh! It's been so long," she said without looking at him. "I thought I'd never come again."

Lily turned to Adam and asked, "I'm not, you're first . . . am I?"

"No, I had a girlfriend and we . . . She . . ."

Lily let out a sigh of relief. "That's okay. I just thought for a second that maybe you were a virgin. You don't have to tell me about it."

Neither one said a word, or moved until she came closer and squeezed Adam tightly. She looked into his eyes, then rested her head on his chest. "That was wonderful," she said into his neck.

FIFTEEN

Adam lay half asleep, hearing himself breathe and expecting to hear the sounds that ordinarily woke him. Back home, there were a series of sounds that queued the different hours of the morning. The neighbor's dog barked at the squirrels first, followed by the garbage truck that dumped a metal bin with a battering sound in the parking lot nearby, right before the sun came up. If that didn't wake him, there was his sister's radio as she got ready for school, followed by either someone in the kitchen slamming a cabinet door or someone in the restroom slamming the toilet seat. On weekends, his sister slept in, but he could hear his father cutting wood on the table saw in the backyard or pounding away with a hammer.

It was mostly dark, and Lily was dressed, milling around the room without making a sound. She noticed Adam looking at her and went to the side of the bed where he lay.

"Sorry," she said softly. "I wake up early to feed the horses. Go back to bed. I'll make you something for breakfast when I get back."

She left the room, closing the door quietly as she stepped into the hall.

Adam heard the hard push of the wedged back door as she went outside.

The nights were warm but not hot, and Adam wondered why Lily would've turned off the AC, as the room felt stuffy. Adam became uncomfortable and pulled the sheets off with a hard jerk. He contemplated getting up but stayed there instead. With a deep breath, he relaxed, staring at the ceiling.

Lily came back once there was light outside and asked Adam why he hadn't gone back to sleep.

"Have you ever thought about getting a ceiling fan?" he asked, still in bed.

"Well, no. Why? Can you do that? One would be nice, I guess. I never really thought of putting one in."

She asked about breakfast, but Adam wasn't that

hungry, so after using the restroom, he met Lily in the kitchen where they had toast with butter and jelly, and fresh coffee. Adam, still sleepy and wearing the same clothes from the day before, watched Lily drink coffee, fully dressed and wide awake.

"Is that a lot of work, keeping horses?" Adam asked.

"Not really. I feed them in the morning, then again in the afternoon before leaving for work."

"Do you ride them?"

"No, not anymore. I used to, but now I just take care of them. When I was younger, I was in rodeos. I used to do barrel racin' and breakaway ropin'," she said in a changed voice. "I won Rodeo Queen once when I was in high school and had my picture in the paper."

"You must be a good rider."

"Thanks. Have you ever been on a horse?" she said, looking puzzled.

"Well, I took a picture on a pony once, when I was a little kid."

"That doesn't count!" She nursed her mug, smiling. "Do you want to see my horses?"

"Sure."

After changing into his only other outfit, Adam

went with Lily outside into the blinding light that reflected off the bright green pasture.

They strolled side by side to the rail fence where Adam could see three horses in the distance.

The large creatures moved gracefully, trotting toward the fence to meet Adam and Lily.

Adam cravenly stood a few feet away but watched as the foremost horse loomed near the fence. He was a glistening dark brown giant with a barrel chest and defined muscles down the sides of his neck. A white snip created a dagger-shaped figure between his nose, and a black forelock waved, touched gently by the slightest breeze.

Lily grabbed the top rail with one hand and the other reached for the horse's muzzle. "This is Dickey," she said.

Dickey pulled away. He flicked his ears and shook his head as if to say 'no'. The horse's large, dark eyes studied Adam.

"Do you want to touch him?" she asked.

Adam kept his distance. "Not right now," he said, staring back at the horse.

"The gray one is Gray."

Gray was the spotted horse Adam first saw when Lily had showed him her stable. He stood directly in front of Adam. Up close, his coat was dappled white with solid gray around his front and hind legs. Gray whinnied and tossed his head back as he wiggled his black lips with bristly whiskers.

Lily faced the gray horse. "This is the one I ride—well, last time I rode. He's real gentle."

Gray trotted away, swishing his tail while Dickey stayed near the fence with his head low. Adam could smell his hide, and while it didn't smell too bad, it was a strong, lingering odor that tickled his nose.

"The one over there," Lily said, pointing to the horse farther way, "is Red."

"Where do you come up with their names?"

She laughed. "Those are just their names." She pointed again. "Red is the one I'm going to put in the stable in the evenings. He was my riding horse when I used to perform."

Adam watched Red. He looked haggard with a protruding pelvis bone and spine, and stood with his head low, paying them no attention.

"Those are my horses." Lily rested her elbows on the rail fence and hitched a foot on the bottom rail.

"I can see what you mean about Red . . . about him being skinny," Adam said, remembering their conversation when he agreed to fix the stable.

"Yeah, he's probably only got a short while left in

him. He seems to be eating okay, but I don't know for sure. I think it's his age. Old horses just look that way."

They turned around and went back to the house.

Lily told Adam to relax, so he sat down to watch television as she began to pick up the house a little.

A short while later, she sat next to him on the couch and fiddled with her hair. She appeared to be in a daze, staring at the television, twirling the same lock of hair over and over.

Adam thought about what her life was like, her life before he met her, and he turned to face Lily. There were several questions he wanted to ask, but feared they would remain mysteries for now, as he didn't know where to start, or how to bring them up—not without potentially hurting her feelings, and that was the last thing he wanted to do. He turned away.

"What?" she said with a cute smile.

"Can I ask you something?"

Her smile turned into a serious look fraught with concern. "Yeah."

"Can I ask about your marriage? Why you divorced?"

She gazed down, letting her hair fall to the sides of her face, and stayed that way for a moment, picking her head up again before she forced a smile, then began talking.

"Brian—my ex-husband—and I went to the same high school. We didn't know each other at first. He's from another town, but both towns share the same high school.

"He came up to me one day at the rodeo. I was performing that day; I'd just won 'queen', so I'd become a little popular. I was in fliers and promos." She thought for a moment, smiling. "Anyway, he asked me out and we started dating.

"Everyone liked him; he was tall, handsome, had a gorgeous smile. His daddy owned a lumberyard, so they were doing okay. Well, after high school, I hadn't put much thought into college and my daddy died that summer. I was eighteen. The next year, my mom went to live with my grandmother, to take care of her, and I was left with the house. So we got married."

Lily slipped out of her boots and crossed her legs. She pushed back strands of hair behind her ear and picked at the seam of her jeans. "After we got married, he found out another girl he'd been dating got pregnant.

"Everything was okay at first. I told him we'd work it out. When the baby was born, he would bring him around sometimes, and on his first birthday, Brian went to his birthday party and didn't come back that night. I knew then it would be over. He came home the next day and basically explained that he married me by mistake and he wanted to be there for his son, and that it wasn't my fault. So we divorced."

She wiped the corners of her eyes, then looked at Adam and smiled. "I'm sorry." She sniffed. "I never talk about that. I hope it doesn't upset you."

"Me? No. I asked because I couldn't understand why someone would've divorced you. I figured maybe you divorced him."

"You're sweet."

A terrible sense of guilt came over Adam, who decided not to mention her marriage again.

They spent the next few days enjoying each other's company. During the day, they would talk endlessly and then she'd leave for work in the evenings. Adam even helped feed the horses and her dog, Taylor.

People drove for miles to eat at the quaint little restaurant, K's kitchen. It was the only thing between two small towns and was famous for steak and burgers. There was a small salad bar, but mostly its patrons desired meat. The walls were decorated with old knickknacks and antique store signs. Right near the entrance was a mint 1950s gas pump, and a row of perfectly maintained peddle cars were on display on the wall behind the register. At the front of a long hallway that led to the kitchen was a glass case with florescent lights where rows of plump raw steaks in different sizes were ready to be seared. In the far corner was the desert bar which had a selection of plates, some with large slices of homemade chocolate cake, chunky servings of peach cobbler, or banana pudding with whipped cream.

Lily stood at the register. She rang up an elderly couple, then seated the elderly man who had been waiting. The hunched-over man in overalls leaned carefully on his cane and made small talk with Lily as they walked.

"How are you, beautiful? You know, I won't be available forever—I'll be lucky to be alive noon tomorrow."

Katherine Davis, also known as Kat or 'K', was an elegant lady with bright lipstick and primed, short hair. Each arm was heavily decorated in gold rings and bracelets. The waitresses called her Kat, and she was a good boss, usually pretty lenient about schedules, and she liked waiting on tables and chit-chatting with her regular customers. Lily did some of the bookkeeping. She paid bills and counted money on the evenings she worked. If they were short on help, like tonight when one of the girls didn't have a ride to work, Lily ran the register and seated the customers.

That afternoon, Lily had been cheerful, smiling, and even flirted back with the lewd old man who came in earlier, something she didn't regularly do. Her laughs were heartfelt and resonant, and Kat came over to ask why.

"You seem in a good mood," said Kat. She stood poised against the register, studying Lily's face.

"Can I tell you something?"

Before Kat could answer, a couple walked in.

Lily turned, excited to see the pair of strangers, and walked them to a nearby booth. She walked back to the register and decided she wasn't going to tell anyone about Adam yet. What did she care? After all, she was happy.

The whole drive home, Lily thought about Adam. When she walked in, she didn't even stop to say 'hi'; she went straight for his pants, undid them, and they made love on the living room floor.

* * *

Later in the week, Lily drove Adam out to the building supplies store where he helped her pick out a ceiling fan.

Adam felt like a pro as he entered the electrical section and got a few things he would need. He planned on installing it in her bedroom on Saturday.

Having noticed it tucked away beside the fridge, Adam found a stepstool Lily kept. There were paint stains on the steps from where it had been used before. It wasn't a six-foot ladder like he would've preferred, but she had standard eight-foot ceilings found in older homes.

Lily was out running errands, and Adam had moved the bed where he could get to the light fixture.

Adam found the breaker box in the spare bedroom closet and switched off the bedroom power. He walked over, tried the light, and it was dead.

It was a hard reach, but he managed to unscrew the small fixture and let it dangle as he loosened the wires.

The box lay open to one side, and Adam quickly

assembled the blades and installed the opaque glass fixtures, and in a few minutes the fan was ready to go. While at the store, Adam had explained to Lily that a ceiling fan that rested directly on the ceiling would look better than the ones that hung lower. Now, using only a stepstool, he would struggle a little more to install it.

Adam tied the wires and covered the exposed ends with wire nuts; he crammed the wires as best he could and installed the ceiling fan.

It looked good and it came on when Adam tried switch. The room was strikingly brighter, and Adam could see a thin crack stretching from the corner of a window up to the ceiling with the hint of a shadow permeating the fine line, making it appear worse. The furniture looked pallid, and a cobweb flitted in the corner with the air from the fan.

Adam put the bed back in place, using the indentations on the carpet that marked its original position.

Across the house, Adam could hear Lily's truck coming up the driveway.

She backed in fast, confident with her ability in maneuvering such a large vehicle. There was a round bale of hay strapped into the bed where it appeared enormous in comparison to the truck.

The door slammed shut as she got out.

Adam stood outside and watched.

"Hey," she said.

Adam snickered, looking at the round hay bundle.

Lily lowered the tailgate and climbed up.

"Do you need help?" Adam asked coyly.

"Nah." She unhooked an orange strap, then jumped off and walked to the small building near the house Adam had assumed was a garage. Lily pulled two wide doors apart and went inside.

"Can you undo the tube gate?" she asked from inside the darkness.

A long bar separated the driveway from the yard, and Adam unlatched it, then walked the cumbersome gate toward the house.

Lily drove out of the small building on a tractor, or what appeared to be a smaller version of one. The blue tractor had exhaust pipes near the front, along with smaller wheels near the engine and large, rutted wheels near the seat. An awning covered the seat, but it had no glass, and she rode with the hydraulic arms raised, pulling levers and handles.

A set of forks on the arms bent forward as she

drove slowly, digging the forks into the round bale. The arms boomed down and the round bale turned. The truck rose with a bounce once it was relieved of the weight.

The tractor's engine sputtered as Lily backed out and carried the bale several feet off the ground. She drove into the yard, all the way to the rail fence where she kept the horses. Her tractor dwindled into the distance as she headed for the entrance to the horse pen.

Once she reached the pen, Lily eased the bale of hay into a hay ring—a round, cage-like cylinder that kept the hay in one place.

Adam waited near the tube gate until she returned. He could smell the exhaust as he walked behind the tractor and watched Lily drive back onto the driveway. She turned the tractor and backed into the building, lowering the forks close to the ground as she cleared the entrance.

She closed the large doors to the building and Adam hitched the tube gate back in place.

"I've got something in the truck," she said, and walked over to the passenger side. She returned with a plastic department store bag.

They went inside.

Adam was eager to show Lily the fan.

Lily set the bag onto the couch. "Come here, I got you something." She laid out a couple pairs of pants, some shorts, a pack of underwear, and a few t-shirts.

He liked the clothes right away.

"I checked your size last time I washed. I figured you could use some jeans. Do you want to try them on?"

"Yeah, I will. Thanks." Adam looked at her; she appeared genuinely happy. He knew the jeans would fit by looking at them, but for her sake, he went into her restroom to try them on.

When Adam returned with his new clothes on, Lily played with the fan and commented on how much brighter it was. She circled Adam and asked if the jeans fit well.

"They fit great," he said. They were snug, but he had lost a little weight too, so he figured he'd be fine.

The following day, Adam made love to Lily before she left for work. After she left, he wandered around the house with nothing to do and stopped to skim through a few paperbacks on the bookshelf in the living room. They were old books with worn covers and tinged, golden pages. The covers indicated they were Westerns, as most of them had cowboys on them. *Louis L'amour,* Adam read the author's name. He pulled a few of the books down and looked inside one.

Adam didn't expect to read about a stranded Air Force pilot in Alaska at a time when Russian sailors were heavily present for the sake of a lucrative fur trade. That evening, Adam read half the book in one sitting, more than he'd ever read at one time.

The evening bestowed the night.

Lily arrived and told Adam about her day.

Adam sat watching her as she talked about something funny that happened at the restaurant. One of the waitresses had been in a hurry and grabbed a pair of jeans out of the drier, threw them on and came to work. It turned out that a pair of her panties had been inside the pants and she'd drug them around on the bottom of her pants leg and didn't realize until the end of her shift. When she noticed, she'd been so embarrassed, she bent down, scooped them up, and shoved them into the nearest trash can. Lily burst out laughing.

Adam couldn't help but notice the way her breasts quavered and her stomach muscles contracted when she laughed. He succumbed to her beauty as being the most amazing thing, and carefully studied every detail about her.

Adam loved her.

He loved her, not just because she was beautiful and did nice things for him. That was essential, but he loved wanting her; wanting to take her in moments like these, and wanting to be inside her more than anything.

They made love that evening in a slow and passionate way and Adam took great pleasure in the things she allowed when they were interacting in foreplay, squeezing his hand into her pants and touching the soft, sultry area at the base of her pelvis and caressing the rest of her body.

Times he'd tried stimulating Michelle, even while they were both nude, making out and on the verge of intercourse, she would scorn him and say something along the lines of, "Uh, excuse me, but that's *my* private."

Adam didn't miss Michelle by any means, and especially not while in bed, holding Lily. If this was what being married was like, then Adam wanted to marry her.

SIXTEEN

It was after breakfast, and Lily washed dishes while humming. She looked up to give Adam a smile, who smiled back before turning to look through the dining room window. He saw Taylor in the field, with his tail up, investigating something on the ground.

A few days had passed since the furry little scamp had come by, so Adam went to see him.

Taylor didn't run toward Adam as he came near; he simply watched.

Adam knelt beside him and raked his fingers through Taylor's husky, black mane, then impulsively tugged hard at Taylor's ear and patted the side of his muzzle just to see what he would do. Taylor stiffened with a jump and watched Adam from a side glance. Adam stood, then took a step back. The dog leapt forward, nipping at Adam's hands, then stopped and watched Adam move backward, one step after another. Taylor continued biting playfully and the banter between them turned into a friendly tussle.

A while later, Taylor gave up and trotted over to the back porch where he found a cool, shaded spot next to the house and collapsed. His tongue lolled out, and the sides of his mouth were frothy as he lay there panting and noisily lapping up the drool.

Adam went back inside, and as he closed the door, he looked into the living room where he found Lily chatting on the phone. She sat on the couch with her legs crossed while her free hand rested on a knee.

"No," she said, a little agitated. "I haven't talked to Uncle David. I haven't talked to Aunt Emma, either."

She leaned her head, cradling the phone against her shoulder.

Adam grabbed his book, anxious to finish it, and stretched out on the opposite couch trying to find his place in the story.

"I'm just out here, taking care of the house," she said. "How is Lee, anyway?"

Lily listened.

"Well, if he can afford it. No, he never calls me either, Momma! I know. Well, he knows where I live. He's welcome to stay here any time."

She talked a few more minutes before hanging up.

Adam set the book down on his waist and asked

whom she'd just spoken to, ascertaining if it had in fact been her 'momma'.

Lily had called her mother, who had asked if she'd heard from a few of their relatives. Lee was her younger brother who had basically inherited a piece of land her father had left behind. Lee worked for a company that leveled land; he was a machine operator and made good money. She described his 'nice house' as one having a large fountain with a U-shaped driveway and spiraling staircase entrance.

"Do you ever see your brother?" Adam asked, though he expected he knew the answer.

"No." She stared at the floor. "He was good friends with Brian and we haven't really seen each other since . . ." She picked at the phone antenna for a moment. "Momma just told me that his youngest daughter is now *three.* I haven't even met that one."

"Wait, didn't you say your name was Laura, Lee?"

"Yeah." She smiled as she considered the question.

"And your brother's name is Lee?"

"Our grandfather was named Lee. Daddy named me Lee first since I'm the firstborn, but when my brother was born, he named him after Grandpa, too."

Adam wondered about her father, but seeing as though Lily had turned the television on and seemed preoccupied by the flickering images, he turned back to his book instead.

Lily had the day off, and in the evening she got up to feed the horses. Adam finished the book with the grandeur of a person fulfilling a great accomplishment, then went to put the book away. He stopped near the window where he looked outside and saw Lily sitting calmly in the rocking chair, staring into the sunset.

Adam put the book on the shelf and went outside.

He said 'hi' to Lily and she gave him her complete attention. Worried about her sitting alone, Adam felt compelled to ask, "Are you okay?"

"Yeah. Everything okay inside? Are you hungry?"

"No, not really. Just checking on you."

To that, she smiled.

Taylor had been nearby, and he raced over and fawned Adam's hand, then sat on the floor next to Lily.

"You want to see a trick?" she asked.

"Okay."

Lily turned back in her chair, reached for the screen door, and said, "Taylor!"

The dog perked up with his ears cocked high on his head.

"Go get my cigarettes," she said.

Taylor bolted into the house and returned in a moment's time with a white box of cigarettes in his mouth. They both laughed, and Lily cooed Taylor over and removed the crushed box from his mouth.

Adam stopped laughing long enough to say, "How did you teach him that?"

"He knows where I keep them, on the dresser, and he learned to find them. Blue heelers know how to do all kinds of stuff. I love that dog!"

Lily reached into her pocket, pulled out a see-through butane lighter, and pulled a cigarette out from the crumpled box.

"Do you mind?" she said, before lighting the cigarette in her mouth.

"No. I didn't know you smoked."

She sat up in the rocking chair, and Adam watched her face light up as the flame from the lighter touched the cigarette. He then took a seat on the porch step and gazed at the blue-orange sky that would be dark soon.

"I usually don't," she said, pulling the cigarette out of her mouth. "I've had this pack forever. Just, sometimes when I come home from work, if I feel real stressed, I'll smoke. But I usually go long times without it."

As she held the smoldering cigarette in one hand, Adam asked, "Do you mind if I have one?"

"No." She handed over the cigarettes and lighter.

Adam lit his and took a light puff, letting the smoke fill his mouth without actually inhaling it. This cigarette had been different from the one he'd tried, and Adam didn't mind it so much because it seemed less harsh. It felt good, in the warm evening, taking in a puff and feeling the smoke against his eyes and up his nose where it stung just a little.

Lily held the cigarette in her mouth, closing one eye as the smoke swirled close to her face. She finished it with one last drag, then stamped the butt out on the porch.

Adam didn't finish his, but he dropped it onto the ground just the same. He felt relaxed. He turned enough that he faced Lily, and asked, "How did your father pass away?"

Lily cleared her gullet as she contemplated the question.

"He had a heart condition," she started to say. "He had surgery for it and seemed okay. When we first found out, we thought he'd had a heart attack. The ambulance came and got him. I remember they gave him something that stopped his heart."

She paused. "He used to talk about it all the time. Then, after he had another incident, the ambulance came again. But that time, they had tried to revive him the whole way to the hospital. He was only fifty-two when he passed."

Adam offered his sincerity, but felt it hadn't helped, so he thought to keep her talking in hope that he hadn't provoked only hurtful memories.

"What was he like?" Adam asked.

"My daddy was kind and intelligent. He could be funny sometimes. He was kind of an old-fashioned cowboy, but a gentleman. He was a good businessman, too. He was a salesman for a long time and bought himself some land. We own eighty acres here, and he has almost thirty on a field where he used to raise cattle, which is where my brother lives now. Then he started a small trucking business to haul gravel.

"When he passed, Momma gave Lee the land with the cattle, but Lee's no rancher, so he sold the cattle to someone, but keeps them on his land and leases the land. It's kind of a smart move because they keep the grass down, and he doesn't have to pay property taxes, *and* someone pays him. Lee was always figuring out a way to make a buck."

Adam noticed how the topic had changed from her father to her brother, and he felt relieved.

Lily stopped talking and the sound of crickets became alive and vibrant.

They sat in the dark now, and while Adam thought there might've been a porch light, it was off. He stood, grabbed Lily by the hand, and said, "Come here."

She got up from the rocking chair and took the steps leading down from the porch. They walked into the dark yard where it seemed impossible to see, but Adam moved forward, tugging Lily close behind with each faithful step. He held her hand until they reached a spot that felt vast and empty.

Being the sky wasn't clear enough to make out any stars, Adam oriented himself using the location of the house, then turned Lily by the shoulders, facing her easterly to a purple sky.

"You can't see it right now," Adam said, "but this time of year, the planet Venus rises in the east right before sunrise. Aside from the moon, it's the brightest thing out there, large and yellow and low in the sky."

"Oh. How do you know this?"

"I took Astronomy in high school," Adam said with assertiveness, not mentioning that he would still be enrolled in the class were he not standing with her now. "The first semester is constellations and the second semester is planets."

"We didn't have Astronomy at my high school," she contended.

"I was always fascinated by Venus," he continued, "more than the other planets because there was so much significance to it and it just seemed to stand out, throughout the ages. Venus is named after the Roman Goddess of beauty, and I used to think there had been a man out there who saw a woman so beautiful that he believed there had to be a goddess just for love.

"Then the Pagans realized that in its orbit, as it crosses Earth, it forms a pagan star."

"What? It orbits in the shape of a star?"

"No, it orbits in a circle, only it rotates the opposite way. Anyhow, at the points where it meets Earth's orbit, it forms a star. So the pagans saw it as a symbol of caring and love, and they associated it as being feminine—kind of making women sacred, which was why they were chosen to bare children."

"Wow," she said in awe.

"I never truly understood it before. I mean, I couldn't understand having such deep feelings for someone—until now." Adam's eyes found hers in the dark night. "I think you are so beautiful . . ." Adam lost his train of thought and searched for something to say. "I can't believe I just met you like this, by accident."

Adam held Lily close. He felt like no one else existed in the world—just the two of them, and the only thing that mattered to him was her. They kissed and it was sensual and spell-binding.

Lily smiled after they pulled away.

"I wish we could stay out here until Venus comes up," she said, looking into the sky.

"It'll be morning before you can see it."

She turned to look at him. "Thank you for making me feel special."

Their clasped hands swung between them as they walked back to the house, and around them the wind began to pick up.

In the middle of the night the rain poured with a deafening sound, thunder boomed and cracked and Adam woke up. He walked over to the window where he could see the downpour, and nothing else. A few uneventful minutes later, he lay back down only to be jolted by an ominous crack of thunder that sounded like the world had ripped apart, leaving behind a whir that echoed across the sky. Once the sound evaded, Adam went back to sleep.

Adam woke up refreshed the next morning and rolled over, expecting to see the half-empty bed. The sun hadn't come up and as Adam got up and went to the kitchen, he could hear the faint drizzle of rain. He went straight to the coffee pot where two fingers touched the scolding glass surface with black liquid inside.

The cups were located in the cabinet above the pot. Adam reached for one, as he had now familiarized himself well with the kitchen. During the last few weeks he learned to like coffee and routinely had a cup each morning. He empirically learned he liked it black.

Lily burst through the back door and the rain sound amplified for the time it took her to close the door again. She was wet, with trails of rain that ran down her face forming droplets on her chin.

Adam held his cup. "Do you need a towel?"

Lily stood near the dining table as she shook her hands, then rubbed water away from her face.

"Yeah, if you wouldn't mind," she said, stooped over with her shoulders hunched.

Adam set the cup down, quickly headed for the restroom, and returned with a towel. Lily had taken off her boots when he returned and she patted herself with the bundled towel.

"Thanks. I was trying to get Red to go into the stable. I remembered when I woke up, but he wasn't wearing a bridle and I couldn't get him to budge."

She threw the towel over her shoulders, then went to the restroom and began to remove her wet clothes.

Adam waited in the living room, sipping lukewarm coffee, staring at the light that emitted from the restroom and filled the hallway. He put his cup down, strolled over, and stood where he could see her.

Lily was wearing only her bra and panties, examining her face in the mirror. She looked over at Adam, completely oblivious to her unrestrictive physical nature.

"Could you be a sweetheart and put some feed in the horse buckets if the rain lets up later?" A towel clung to her hands as she walked over to Adam. She stopped near the restroom doorway, wringing her hair.

"Yeah, sure thing."

"Thanks."

She disappeared into her bedroom.

Adam turned back to the living room and Lily came out in shorts and a t-shirt.

"You want breakfast?" she asked as she passed him on the couch. Adam said yes, and they ate together without saying much.

Lily got dressed and went to work. She pecked Adam on the lips as he lay on the couch, watching television.

Adam made several trips to the window, but it continued to rain through the afternoon.

Around six, the rain abated and Adam went outside. The ground was soaked as Adam clunked over to the stable where he filled a bucket with feed.

With the feed in hand, he made the long trek to the buckets Lily kept nailed to the stanchions inside the pen, high enough for the horses to reach easily.

Lily had instructed him to use a couple of scoops, and Adam poured just enough into each of the buckets. Gray and Dickey traipsed over with their coats darkened by the rain. The ground inside the horse pen was like clay. Each step he made let out a gushing, suction sound, and Adam took several minutes to get back to the gate.

The grass-covered area outside the pen was easier to walk on. The rain began to come down again, and Adam splashed through puddles and waded back to the stable, where he dropped the feed bucket carelessly on the floor, then hurried back to the house.

That evening, the driveway had become a stream as the flurry of rain came down when Lily returned home from work. She ran inside and went to dry off.

Adam had experimented with some spaghetti

which actually turned out well. Lily was impressed with Adam, who had shown no interest in cooking before. The rest of the night was quietly spent in front of the television, and the gloomy weather caused them both to start yawning around 10 p.m., and by 10:30 they were in bed.

The following morning, Adam got up and went for the coffee pot when he almost bumped into Lily, who pushed her way inside quickly through the back door. She was drenched even worse than before as her hair was matted to her face and her wet shirt had molded to her breasts and stomach. With an inert expression on her face, she looked mutely at Adam. They both stood there in a weird silence, then she took a few gushy steps over to the coffee pot. Lily reached for a mug and poured a cup of coffee, then rummaged around for cream and sugar. A pink packet flapped in her hand.

"Red died last night," she said, pouring the sugar into her coffee. She kept her head lowered as a spoon clinked around in her mug. The spoon was set down, and Lily turned around and leaned against the counter, staring into her cup before taking a sip.

"I'm sorry, Lily." Adam remembered he hadn't seen him yesterday afternoon and immediately felt guilty.

"No, it's okay. I should've put him in the stable every night, like I planned."

Lily stood in the kitchen for another arcane

moment, drinking coffee, then passed through the living room to the hallway, where she kicked her mucky boots off, and went to change clothes.

Adam waited, but Lily didn't come back to the living room.

He found her looking out her bedroom window with her mug in hand. Adam walked into the dark bedroom. He'd went to talk to Lily, but she spoke first.

"I can't bury him today, because the ground will be too wet for the tractor."

Adam, who hadn't been fond of or even showed any interest in the horse, felt sad, though he figured it was empathy for Lily. In her sorrow, she had let her friend down.

A couple days passed and it hadn't rained anymore. Lily decided she would try to bury Red. Adam insisted he help, and they went over to the building near the house where Lily kept the tractor.

Lily rode out as Adam held the tube gate open once more. After he closed it, he jogged lightly, catching up to the noisy machine, bouncing along the ride through the clumpy ground.

Lily drove thinking about Red. He'd somehow been her last connection to her father. After all, *he* helped her train him, *he* took her to all the rodeo events, and *he* had named him—with her help. The night her father brought home the horse, Lily was just a little girl, and she heard her father refer to him as 'the red horse'. "Red?" she had said one time, and the name stuck. Now he was gone, and it was all her fault.

Red was lying on his side at the farthermost end of the horse pen. They were so far in that Adam couldn't see the house anymore; it'd become hidden somewhere behind the stable.

The horse's stomach had ballooned enormously, and splatters of mud covered his neck, parts of his chest, and the two legs closest to the ground. The smell was putrid, and Adam tried his best to keep from hurling. He caught a glimpse of Lily, sitting on the tractor, who winced as she spoke.

"Well, at least this is about where I'd put him. I probably wouldn't be able to carry him too far anyway."

The tractor now had a bucket, Lily called it: a scoop that dug large mounds of clotted earth up in slow, unwieldy rips. By the time she finished digging, the hole turned out to be pretty big, and Lily explained that if it wasn't buried deep enough, coyotes and other animals could dig it up.

She brought a chain with her and tied it around the horse's legs so she could use the tractor scoop to pull him up, like the characters in old movies that hung from a pole as they were carried away by natives into a village, but the chain kept coming off, and Adam's attempts to pull or push were useless. Finally, Lily dragged Red by the hind legs where the chain still held, and she managed to get him into the hole.

She covered him with dirt and flattened the ground with the tractor.

They were both now covered with mud as they made their way back.

Lily seemed okay, but Adam would do the best he could to cheer her up.

SEVENTEEN

Saturdays at Lily's were like any other day she worked, only today Adam wanted to take her somewhere fun. While she didn't seem like the outgoing type, there had to be a place she would want to go. Adam wondered why the thought hadn't crossed his mind sooner; it wasn't until he looked into his wallet earlier that afternoon and realized he still had almost $600 of the money he'd earned.

Adam shaved and took a shower, then dressed in the restroom where he put on a fresh pair of jeans and a clean t-shirt. Finally, he splashed on some of the Old Spice aftershave he'd seen in the medicine cabinet. After he finished in the restroom, he went to find his shoes. Adam sat on the couch, waiting for Lily to come home.

Lily arrived just after 9 p.m., and Adam went to

meet her at the front door. She stepped inside, and Adam stood there smiling. He noticed she smelled like food when he went to hug her. She pulled away from him, frowned, and said, "This is a warm welcome. Are you okay?"

"I want to take you out somewhere."

"Like, where? There's nothing around here."

"Oh, I don't know . . . What do you like to do?"

She considered for a moment with a look of uncertainty. "No, you don't have to take me anywhere."

"No, I do! I want to get out of the house for one night, do something fun." Adam threw a shot in the dark. "We can go to a restaurant or go dancing."

Lily laughed. She walked through the formal living room and placed her keys down in the kitchen.

"Okay," she said. "Let's go cut some rug."

"What?"

"Ha, that means dancing."

Lily took a few minutes to freshen up and came out wearing a plaid, short-sleeved shirt and libidinous makeup in the form of dark eye shadow, blush, and red lipstick. Adam checked one more time to make sure his wallet was in place, and Lily grabbed her keys as they headed out the door.

Taylor ran over to the truck as they got in. "Hey boy," she said before she opened the door and jumped in. The dog's soft whining could be heard on the other side of the truck as Adam hopped in as well.

In the dark cab, a jingle of her keys started the truck but Lily turned on the dome lights and searched through her console between the seats where a stack of CDs filled the small compartment.

"Do you like George Straight?" she asked as she popped in the CD.

"Sure," Adam said. It was a lie because he didn't listen to him and hadn't made a fair judgment of his music, but tonight was about Lily, and he couldn't think of anything he'd say no to.

Over the sound of music, a breeze whirred through the truck windows after she'd lowered them just a crack. The music, though, was good—upbeat, and it made Adam want to bob his head. Lily chimed a few bars, but didn't sing the entire song.

The night masked the world around them with only the slightest of things that could be seen along the road, a porch light or the reflectors leading to someone's driveway, and Adam didn't remember the night he'd spent walking the roads to be as dark as they were now.

They reached civilization in the form of a few buildings, street lights, and brightly lit billboards as the truck fared through a commercialized part of town. The drive through was short-lived, and soon their excursion took them on another dark road.

Lily slowed as she approached a distinct red

building with a gable roof that reminded Adam of a barn. On either side of the building were several cars and trucks parked in rows over a gravel parking lot. The lights that marked the entrance lit the way for a group of young couples who appeared to be leaving. Discolored white letters on the side of the building depicted the name IN CAHOOTS. Adam read the cracked and faded letters and naturally saw a business opportunity as he thought to call Ernie one day.

There wasn't a single parking spot available, it seemed, and Lily drove until she passed the last parked truck where she made a half circle and backed in beside it. They both got out and walked along the building where the faint beats of music could be heard through the wall.

"This place is pretty popular," Lily said as they walked. "It's a restaurant during the day, and at night they move all the tables and play music. A lot of people come here to dance or just hang out."

The entrance was dark, but once inside there were neon signs advertising various beers on different walls. A group of people danced in the middle, their figures floating around, interspersed with colorful rotating lights. An ordering window to the side shined light onto the worn dance floor strewn with hay. Lily led the way, walking along the back wall past a few tables until she found one where they could sit.

"Are you hungry?" she said in a raised voice,

speaking over the music.

A solemn-looking woman with a seriousness that came from deep inside her soul came over and took their orders.

"Mind if I have a beer?" Lily asked Adam.

"No," he said. "Go ahead."

The solemn woman had a heavy accent, and her voice could be hard clearly through the music. "And for you, sir?"

"A Coke," he said, not knowing if she would ask for his ID. Adam figured he'd be hungry soon and asked for a menu.

There wasn't one. The waitress shot off four options, and when he asked if the chicken tenders would come with fat-free Ranch, she said, "There's nothin' fat-free in that kitchen."

Adam opted for the quesadilla.

As they had walked in, Adam feared he would be underdressed but there was hardly a person in there with a button shirt on. The persons dancing wore t-shirts and John Deer hats and Adam felt comfortable knowing he wouldn't stand out—not for being underdressed, anyway.

The waitress came and went without saying another word. Lily drank her bottled beer while Adam ate and sipped his cold soda.

Not long afterward, Adam stared at his empty plate and noticed his cup full of ice had been that way for the past couple of songs.

The waitress passed by and Lily shot up an index

finger, like someone with an idea, and the waitress picked up Adam's plate and returned with a beer and a fresh Coke.

After her third beer, Adam asked Lily to dance. She seemed relaxed, and her facial expression bore a lazy smile as she said yes. They reached the dance floor, and as fate would have it, a slow song played in which the two could hold each other and take slow steps, and Adam felt like the song playing had been just for them.

'I love everything about you . . . the things that excite you . . . I just want to hold you forever . . .'

Adam held Lily close to his chest and could smell the alcohol on her breath. He thought about a time when he spoke on the phone with Michelle, and she'd asked, 'What's our song?' Adam didn't have an answer for her, and he didn't like the song she'd suggested, so their decision on a song had remained questionable. Tonight, though, there was no doubt in his mind that the song playing while they danced was *their* song.

By the end of the night, Lily had five beers, Adam counted. It was just after midnight and he asked if she was ready to leave. They got up, and Lily reached for his hand as they walked outside. Adam didn't know if it was because she loved him or because she was drunk, but either way, he wanted to be there for her under any circumstance.

"How about I drive?" Adam offered when they were close to her truck.

"You wanna drive my truck?" She looked at him with that same, lazy smile.

"Yes."

"Okay." She reached into the pocket of her tight jeans and handed him the keys.

There were just a few cars left in the parking lot when they got inside. Adam found it hard to see, driving such a large vehicle, but he soon got used to the feeling. Now, it was just a matter of driving back the way they came, which he found simple enough.

They were down the road when Lily took her seatbelt off. She folded up the console between the seats and slid over to sit right next to him. Her nose and chin rubbed his shoulder, and she placed a hand on his lap. As she leaned against him, he drove bearing a discomfort in his pants.

"Thanks for taking me out. I had fun."

"Me, too."

Adam drove down all the dark roads they had passed earlier and managed to make it to her house without incident. He even managed to park her truck without hitting anything.

They walked inside and Lily undressed in the bedroom where she flopped down on the bed wearing nothing at all. She pulled Adam on top of her when he walked into the bedroom.

They made love slowly, and Adam watched her, lying with her eyes closed, smiling, and every so often hooking a fingertip into her mouth in a sexy way that made Adam want to make her the happiest woman alive.

Sunday morning, Lily fixed breakfast, and as they ate, she told Adam that she'd forgotten to mention last night that she would go into work a little early this morning. It seemed like a short while later that she was dressed and ready to go.

Lily arrived at work around noon.

Kat had stopped Lily Friday night before they were leaving and told her one of the waitresses had quit. None of the girls had quit in a while, and Lily didn't mind covering one of their shifts every once in a while anyway.

Something about working during lunch made her feel out of place, though. She wasn't sure if it was the bright light outside; she was used to seeing the less severe evening sun, or perhaps it was the customers? They were different from the ones who came in around 3 or 4 in the afternoon, around the start of her shift, mostly elderly gentlemen who swooped in to take advantage of the early bird special—even though they always got the discount anyway.

Things were slow for the time of day. In fact, it had been over an hour since a customer walked in.

Lily found herself staring out the window when she felt someone come in. She turned to see Brian standing at the door.

Brian smiled as he made the short walk to the

register. "Hello, Laura," he said in his low drawl that struck Lily with a piercing feeling.

All the times Lily had asked him to call her 'Lily', he'd refused to call her something so 'childish'. She sighed. He looked good; he hadn't gained any weight, and his face looked exactly the same as she remembered it. He had handsome, short hair, and wore a new-looking polo shirt he'd tucked into his jeans that fit snug around his thick legs.

She grimaced. "What are you doing here?"

"I'm here to see you."

"I'm at work. I can't talk to you right now."

Brian went behind the register, got close to her, and put his hands on her shoulders, rubbing them slowly. "Relax. I just wanted to see you." He softened his tone. "You can take a break, can't you?"

Kat went over to Lily and Brian. "I can watch the register if you have someone here to see you," she said, smiling at Brian, who smiled back.

Lily walked away without so much as saying 'thanks', and Brian followed her to a nearby booth. They sat down and watched each other across the table.

"Okay," Lily said, sounding fierce. "What is it?"

"I just wanted to see you . . . Everything okay with you?"

"Since when do you care? I've been living on my own for THREE years," she said, agitated.

His head bowed in shame, but he quickly looked

up again and stared into Lily's eyes. "I'm sorry, Laura. I never apologized for what I did, but I thought I was doing the right thing; I was trying to be there for Travis. For my son."

"I understand."

"But I didn't mean to hurt you, Lily. I still love you."

Lily looked away. She didn't want him calling her Lily, and she didn't want to believe he still loved her. "Well, it's a little too late now."

"Lily, things haven't worked out like I expected. I thought she was the one, but then I realized she wasn't. We fight all the time, no joke. And I realized I fight with her because I'm trying to make her you. I realized that, Lily. I realized I love you . . . Had Travis not been born, we'd be living together right now, with children of our own!" Brian had raised his voice. He reached over and touched her hands. Lily pulled hers away with a gasp.

"I can't, Brian."

"Look, I messed up . . . I messed up. Things can't be the way they were, but I want to win you over. I'll do whatever it takes to show you I love you."

Lily looked at him with skepticism. Brian had never talked like that before. He was the boss's son and was used to just barking out orders.

"Not right now . . ." she said, full of sorrow.

"Alright. But I'm not quitting. I'm going to show you that you were meant to be my girl."

"I have to get back to work."

"Okay. I've taken up enough of your time. Just wanted to let you know how I felt. I'll be seeing you. I promise."

Lily got up, as did Brian, and she stood there as he hugged her, sad and not nearly convinced. Then he left.

The rest of the night, she was short with her customers and sneered at one of the waitresses for asking to make change at the register several times throughout the night. Lily was the last one to leave. She got into her truck and cried the entire way home.

Lily had the day off on Wednesday, but spent most of the day outside. She fed the horses and combed them. The hay ring got raked and she even walked over to where Red had been buried, to see if any animals had dug up his carcass.

In the evening, she came to the house, but she sat on the porch, waiting for the sun to go down.

Adam hadn't seen Lily all day. He wondered where she was, and spotted her when he went to look outside. Being sad was hard, and Adam knew first-hand that sometimes a person just needed to get over things, but he decided to go outside to see if she wanted to talk.

"Hey, Lily."

She looked up at him and her eyes appeared red, like she'd been crying. He knelt to hug her, but she only sat there, motionless, staring at some place between her boots and the porch steps.

"Are you still sad about Red?"

"No."

"Is there anything I can do to cheer you up?"

"I don't need cheering up!" She got up and went inside.

Adam went inside and found her door closed. He watched television for a couple of hours, then crawled into bed with Lily after she'd fallen asleep.

The following night, when Lily came home from work, she stormed in and stood in front of Adam, who lay on the couch watching a funny sitcom.

"Don't you get tired of watching television all day?" she said in an angry tone, one Adam had never heard before.

He sat up. "Are you okay?"

"I'm okay, but every day I come home, you're just on the couch watching television. Is that all you do?"

Adam didn't move from the couch. Embarrassed, he remained silent.

Lily yelled in frustration, something else he'd never heard her do, and just to make sure he understood she was upset, she slammed the bedroom door.

The television show suddenly wasn't interesting anymore. Adam sat there and stared at the figures on the screen, but he didn't care for what he was watching. It was 1 a.m. and Adam felt his stomach growl. He strolled over to the fridge where he pulled a couple slices of sandwich meat out with the tips of his fingers and chomped them down.

Adam brushed his teeth and turned the living room light off, then fell asleep on the couch without a pillow or a blanket.

"Adam . . ." a woman's voice whispered.

Adam woke up and saw Lily staring at him, her face close to his.

"I'm sorry about last night," she said and kissed him on the cheek. "Sorry, sweetie, I'm making you something to eat right now." She leaned in, hugged him tightly and went off to the kitchen.

Things seemed they had gone back to normal.

EIGHTEEN

Adam woke up early the following Friday. Assuming Lily was outside routinely feeding the horses he went to the kitchen and smiled at the thought of surprising her with an omelet. The windows along the formal living room glowed with soft light and while the kitchen lights remained off, Adam didn't need them to see. He brought out a frying pan and some eggs and butter out of the fridge, then turned one of the knobs on the stove, adjusting the cheap plastic dial to medium. After setting the pan down on the stove he went back to the fridge and found some ham and cheese.

Over the hissing sound of melting butter, Adam heard a voice outside. The voice came from the front of the house and Adam stepped into the formal living room where he peeked through the veil curtains and saw Lily standing in front of someone. She remained in one spot; her back was to the house, but Adam could see her arms were crossed.

Parked on the driveway behind Lily's truck was a red truck that glistened brightly under the morning sun. Behind Lily was a man, talking, and nodding after every few words. He was tall with dark hair parted to one side, dark eyebrows, and a wide grin. The man then bowed his head low as he spoke and looked directly at her. Adam thought he saw her nod and then she started back toward the house. The man turned toward the truck and hit the alarm button, unlocking the door.

Lily was climbing the steps when Adam hurried back to the kitchen. The frying pan had begun to smolder, and he lifted it to abate the heat.

As the door opened, Adam heard the sound of the truck's engine as it backed out, but he pretended not to hear anything as he cracked a few eggs into a bowl.

Lily walked around to the hallway that led to her bedroom, avoiding the kitchen. Adam continued cooking and set the coffee pot.

The eggs came out nicely; they were a light yellow color and evenly cooked, free of the dark burned spots Adam hated so much. Adam looked admiringly at the two omelets as they had turned out the same size, then he neatly placed pieces of toast halves to one side of each plate. He set the plates down on the dining table with accompanying silverware.

Adam paused near the dining table, viewing his breakfast presentation before he went to fetch Lily.

Careful not to barge in, Adam opened the door slowly. "Lily?" he called out before walking in. She lay on the side of the bed, the side she normally slept on, and was curled up with her hands between her knees.

"I made breakfast," he said.

Lily didn't answer; she only stared at the windows with closed curtains that had been unremittingly drawn apart each morning.

Adam moved closer to her. She looked at him, then got up, adjusted her shirttail with a few tugs, and walked past Adam. For a moment he stood there wondering why she'd been acting so strangely again and he let out a sigh of frustration.

Adam left the room and found her sitting at the dining table, staring at her plate as she rested her chin on the heel of her palm. When he got closer to dining room she got up and poured herself a cup of coffee. She dodged him, when Adam went to pour his own cup and sat down hard into her chair with her cup in hand. Adam took his cup and sat down to eat.

They didn't speak one word to each other. Adam kept watching her, trying to start up a conversation, but she only stared at the slender omelet on her plate, which didn't seem that great anymore, Adam thought, looking at his own.

Lily sipped her coffee. She picked up the fork and ate a small piece of her omelet. She ate another, then a third. She set the fork down and brought the mug close to her, nestled between her hands.

Adam ate all but one bite and looked up from his plate when she said, "Sorry, I'm not that hungry," and got up.

The chore of picking up the dishes took just a couple of minutes, and when he went to place them in the sink, he even washed them—something he'd never done back home.

Alone in the living room, Adam thought of something to say, but couldn't think of anything, so he sat on the couch, waiting, hoping she would come out, sit beside him, and open up about what bothered her. Adam may have been young, be he understood that sometimes people became upset at their loved ones, and arguing back wasn't the answer. Actually, showing someone their loved means letting them have their bad days sometimes.

It seemed like a long time had passed when Adam finally decided to take a shower. Adam scratched his greasy hair as he walked into the restroom. He took his clothes off and let the water run into the bathtub. The water was hot and steamy, and the sound of the shower head seemed deafening as he stood underneath it, letting the water run down his back. While he didn't want to get out, he finished showering, then got dressed.

Adam went into the bedroom, but Lily was gone. She'd be getting ready for work soon and was probably feeding the horses. He walked barefoot into the living room and stood near the television where he could see out through the window.

His eyes scanned the open field and saw nothing, then he noticed her sitting on the rocking chair; it had been pulled over to the side of the porch, but he could see her clearly.

Adam took a few steps toward the back door and paused. A sensation came over him, and he could feel the nervousness boiling inside, unsettling his stomach.

The doorknob turned and Adam pulled open the back door.

Lily was slumped down in the rocking chair, facing the same direction she did in the evenings when she'd watch the sunset. Adam knelt beside Lily and looked directly at her, placing his hands on the chair's armrest.

"Hey, Lily . . ."

Lily looked at him with a sideways glance.

"Could I talk to you?" he asked.

A bird warbled somewhere far away as she remained motionless, now staring at the floor. Adam couldn't deny it any further and asked the inevitable.

"It's me, isn't it?"

Lily gave a look of bewilderment, and Adam watched her carefully, searching for the truth buried deep inside her eyes.

"Does this have something to do with the man who was here earlier?" he asked.

She raged. "Look! I made a big mistake, and now I have the chance to fix it—okay?"

"What about . . . us?"

"Please, Adam. You think I don't have feelings for you? Don't make it harder than it has to be."

* * *

Lily sat quietly, staring off into the mid distance with not a single breeze present to disturb a mesh of hair on her head, and not a single bird in the outlying trees to tweet or warble. On the outside she was Lily, but on the inside she felt hollow, like a creature with no soul.

She avoided making eye contact with Adam kneeling beside her. The truth was, Brian was the love of her life. The one man to which all men she'd ever meet would be compared to. Brian—the one man she'd been truly happy with and was proud to call her own. Though she knew he had been gone, deep inside, she always had hope—even now.

Adam stared at Lily, wanting to see the woman who had been so close and loving, and he wished with all his power that she could somehow snap out of whatever she was going through. It felt as if he were looking at her through foreign eyes, and her facial features, her figure, her hair, her clothes now belonged to just another woman.

"Do you want me to leave?"

Waiting for her answer, Adam felt his eyes well up. He blinked and heard a tear as it plopped softly onto his jeans.

"I'm sorry!" she said.

Lily jumped out of her seat and took one big step off the porch and fled across the yard, and Adam watched. He wanted to run after her, grab her, turn her around and kiss her hard on the lips, but his attempt would be made in vain as he knew she didn't want that. After a few unworldly seconds, Adam turned around and went inside.

The house that once felt bright and alive now felt stale and inanimate.

Adam found his backpack in Lily's bedroom. The drawer he'd used to keep his clothes held just one t-shirt and a pair of socks. Other than the clothes he wore, it was all he would take as the rest was probably in her hamper. Adam put on his shoes and stopped to place his wallet in his back pocket. He thought of grabbing his toothbrush from the restroom, but just walked past it instead, into the dark and now cold-feeling formal living room where he opened the front door and left.

The road was empty, and Adam headed west as he walked under the sun.

NINETEEN

Adam paid little attention to the fields and rows of planted crops as he walked on the dirt edge of the two-lane road. Life seemed to have frozen, as there were no persons outside, and the first car didn't pass him until long after he started walking.

Farther up the road was the motel and the small shopping strip he'd been to, where now there seemed to be no activity whatsoever. The ten-mile hike didn't leave Adam feeling tired, though he certainly looked the part as his face lacked emotion and his gait had been reduced to a trudge. Adam passed the gas station he'd frequented during his stint at the motel and ended up at the shopping strip across from it.

He looked over at the motel, which seemed to

have aged by ten years, with more cracks throughout the walls and more pieces of plaster missing from the small wall outside the motel office, where he'd sat and waited for Ernie. While Adam had enough money to stay there a night, the thought of staying in a sullen room by himself was too depressing.

At the end of the shopping strip was a payphone he'd seen before. Adam made change at the barbeque place he'd bought food from, what seemed like another lifetime ago.

Standing in front of the payphone, Adam pushed a few quarters in and dialed 411, phone directory. He asked for a cab to pick him up at the motel, as he could remember the address there well enough—the dispatcher said it would be an hour.

Adam stepped off the ledge of the shopping strip walkway and realized he was walking through a long shadow cast by the building and severed as an indication of how late it was. He walked across the street where he could wait at the motel, sitting on the low cement wall outside the office.

It was probably 8 p.m. The sun was still out, but it hung low, when a gray-colored sedan with a woman driver pulled into the motel parking lot and asked Adam if he'd called for a cab.

Adam went over and got into the crammed back seat, where his knees rubbed against the vinyl pocket that hung down holding the taxi credentials. He closed the door.

"Where ya headed?" The driver looked at him through the rearview mirror with her clear, bright eyes set deep into a pudgy face with excessive makeup on.

"I'd like to go to the bus station."

The lady reached for her sun visor, pulled out an old Mapsco book, and thumbed through a few pages.

She turned to look back. "It's going to be over thirty dollars."

"That's fine."

The driver put the book down on the passenger seat, then drove away.

Adam stared at the seat in front of him the whole way, ignoring the orange sky and expansive fields he would never see again. The drive wasn't far; thirty minutes had passed when they arrived at the square-shaped building with a rusty awning to one side. It was the bus station, located directly across from the highway.

There wasn't a sign outside or even a single bus. There was a mechanic's garage next door, which shared the building, and in front of the garage doors were several cars that needed repair.

The cab driver stayed back from the building, far enough that she could turn around in the large parking lot. Adam paid her in the form of two twenties, leaving a tip of ten dollars. The backpack in Adam's hand weighed nothing, but he flung it onto his back anyway and walked over to where groups of people were gathered outside the entrance of the building.

Adam walked inside where a few chairs lined one of the walls, occupied by persons with suitcases, and across from them was a single counter near the entrance, giving the room a narrow, hall-like feeling. There was no one at the counter, and Adam went over and waited for the woman with glasses and dark hair to come over.

The woman smiled politely as Adam asked for a ticket, but the last bus going to his destination was sold out.

"The next bus leaves at 8 a.m.," she said with a lilt.

Adam bought the ticket for the morning bus and asked where he could find the restroom. The woman at the counter pointed to the far end, where the room led to a dark hallway.

The moment Adam closed the door to the single-stall restroom, he felt the waterworks want to come on. He stood in front of the mirror where he could see his face, shiny from the oil and sweat, and he gave his disheveled hair a few strokes.

Adam turned the faucet on and splashed water on his face, then cried into the porcelain sink with the water still running full blast. He shut the water off and looked at his eyes; there was no hiding their unpleasant redness. After he wiped them a few times with the sleeve of his shirt, he used the restroom and then left, letting the restroom door shut hard as he went back through the dark hallway.

Outside, the sun had been tucked away, and the last of the orange sky was yet to die out. A bus now sat idling to one side, and Adam could see the destination on the upper corner of the windshield that read EL PASO. The orange lights glowed bright against the imminent nightfall.

Behind one of the groups of people, Adam spotted a payphone standing solemnly at the corner of the building. He strolled over, reached into his pocket where he had a few more quarters left over from the change he'd made earlier, and picked up the phone.

It was past nine o'clock, and Adam's mother would be going to bed soon. He dialed home and waited as the phone rang.

She cleared her throat. "Hello?"

"Mom . . ."

"Oh my God! Adam, where have you been?" she said, sounding panicked, and Adam heard her sniffing in the background. "Are you okay?"

"Yeah, I've been living with this girl, but she doesn't want to be with me anymore. Can I come home?"

"Yes! Do you need money?"

"No, I can buy a bus ticket, but it doesn't leave until tomorrow morning."

"Well, is there somewhere you can stay tonight?"

"No, I can wait at the bus station. There's other people waiting here, too."

"Then come home." They both remained silent for a moment, then she spoke again. "I'll have your father pick you up, when you get here."

Adam said he'd call her, and they said goodbye.

The groups of people had disappeared. Adam leaned against the base of a parking lot light where bugs had formed a small cloud, swarming above him. Several cars passed by on the service road Adam stared into, but none were Lily's white truck.

The voice in his head spoke clearly as Adam was engaged in deep thought.

I lost the best thing to ever happen to me. Yes, but now you have to let go; it wasn't meant to last and fighting it will only make it worse. Things are different now, and that's what you'll have to accept.

Doug's voice joined the conversation, a memory he had from one time when Adam had been angry about something.

'Why are you pissed?' Doug had said. Adam couldn't remember what it was now, but he remembered Doug had scolded him. *'Adam, don't be a sore loser,' he'd said. 'You've got to man up!'*

The thought brought a smile to Adam's face, where he felt a couple tears run down his cheeks. He didn't care who was watching him, but he blinked a few times and held them back.

The rest of the night Adam spent his time staring at the dirt and gravel until the sun came up over the horizon. Although he felt hungry and his mouth was dry, he sat and waited.

The first bus that arrived was headed for Nevada, and it was mostly empty when it left. Inside the bus, the fluorescent lights showed only a few heads near the large, square windows as it drove off.

Adam's bus arrived and it seemed to take forever

to board. As he stood, he felt his butt hurt from sitting on the base of the light post all night. People started forming a line and Adam waited about twenty minutes as they boarded all the passengers.

The bus remained parked for another while as Adam sat in his seat, breathing in the cool air that escaped from the vent below the window where he rested his head. As much as he wanted not to think about his days spent with Lily, it was impossible not to.

Finally, the bus made its way onto the road and shifted gears as it gradually sped up. Adam looked out the window, but the bright morning light hurt his sensitive eyes that felt heavy and tired. The last thing he remembered as he crossed his arms and slumped down was the sound of the bus droning as he sunk into a thoughtless sleep.

TWENTY

The bus jerked and bounced once it made its way through the streets of downtown. Adam opened his eyes, still feeling tired. He yawned and sat up. Soon they arrived at the long parking lot where he'd started his journey not long ago.

The bus station was full of people inside sitting in chairs and standing in all directions. Near the vending machines was a change machine where Adam turned a dollar into quarters. He went outside and found a nearby phone to call his mother, letting her know he'd made it back.

A half hour later, his father's distinctively noisy truck pulled up to the curb, and Adam walked over and jumped inside. Considering he'd left without notice, Adam expected a lecture, but his father didn't say anything resembling a reprimand; instead, he looked at him and with alcohol on his breath, said, "Hi, Adam."

"Hi, Dad."

"Your mom told me you were living with a girl?" He drove away, passing several buildings.

"Yeah, sorry I ran away."

"It's okay. You don't worry about that girl, okay?"

They didn't say anything after that.

Back home, Adam got off the truck; his father said he had somewhere to go.

Before Adam could open the door, Victoria opened it and lunged at him. "Adam! I missed you . . . I'm glad you're back."

Victoria appeared older, her hair was short now, but her shorts were still too small.

Adam went inside and the house was sparkling clean. The sound of something boiling came from the kitchen, and Adam's mother came out smiling. She hugged him hard.

"Hi, baby. Are you glad to be back?" she said, wiping the corner of her eye. "Did your dad tell you about your room?"

"No," he said.

"Go look at it."

Adam started to leave when he stopped and said, "Mom, could you make some coffee?"

"You want coffee? Sure."

The door had been closed, and Adam opened it and walked inside. The room was completely transformed; the walls were painted and he could see an actual plug beside his dresser. It had soft, gray carpet, and Adam looked up and saw a new ceiling fan. There was a new desk near the window where Adam saw his old lamp and computer.

He took a deep breath, and went to lay on his bed which now had a new comforter set on it. The new pillow was soft against his face and Adam lay there before turning to look at the ceiling.

If there were a time in one's life when they found themselves having transitioned from a boy to a man, for Adam, his trip to Abilene had been just that. Adam owed his life to Lily, and even though she'd decided to end their relationship, he would always care about her.

www.ingramcontent.com/pod-product-compliance
Lightning Source LLC
Chambersburg PA
CBHW020335180626
46812CB00001B/223

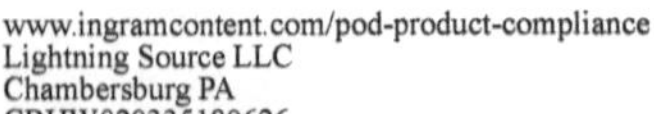

* 9 7 8 0 6 9 2 4 0 6 4 5 8 *